❦ BOOK REVIEWS

ESPECIALLY FOR GIRLS® Presents

Mad,
Mad Monday

Herma Silverstein

Lodestar Books   E. P. Dutton   New York

Edited for Weekly Reader Books and published by arrangement with E. P. Dutton, a division of Penguin Books USA Inc. Especially for Girls and Weekly Reader are federally registered trademarks of Field Publications.

Library of Congress Cataloging in Publication Data

Silverstein, Herma.
    Mad, mad Monday / Herma Silverstein.—1st ed.
        p.   cm.
    "Lodestar books."
    Summary: In trying to cast a spell with a love potion designed to bewitch handsome but conceited Stormy, fourteen-year-old Miranda actually conjures up the ghost of a boy who died in 1958.
    ISBN 0-525-67239-7
    [1. Ghosts—Fiction.   2. Magic—Fiction.]   I. Title.
PZ7.S5877Mad   1987
[Fic]—dc19   87-21287
                                                                    CIP
                                                                    AC

Published in the United States by E. P. Dutton, 2 Park Avenue, New York, N.Y. 10016, a division of NAL Penguin Inc.

Published simultaneously in Canada by Fitzhenry & Whiteside Limited, Toronto

Editor: Rosemary Brosnan   Designer: Barbara Powderly

Printed in the U.S.A.   W   First Edition
10 9 8 7 6 5 4 3 2

my special thanks to
Terry's Group,
the Ladies of Eve,
and Millicent Ames

with love to Terry Dunnahoo,
my picky picky mentor

A Stormy Beginning

1

"A cemetery is just like any other place, Linda Sue."

"Not at midnight, it isn't." Linda Sue sprawled on my bed, her long, thin legs just touching the end. "You've gotten me into some crazy schemes, Miranda, but this time count me out."

"Why? Are you afraid of ghosts?"

She rolled her eyes. "I meant we could get mugged."

"In a cemetery?" I took *Madame Lulu's Book of Magic Spells and Incantations* off my bookshelf and found the love spell I'd marked. "Just think of Dreamland Cemetery as if it were a park. You know, trees, grass, statues . . ."

"Graves."

I shuddered, then plopped on my other twin bed and tried to look confident. "I thought you didn't believe in ghosts."

"Give it up, Miranda. No love spell ever invented will make Stormy Kincaid fall in love with you."

Just hearing Stormy's name sent butterflies zooming around my stomach. "All we have to do is sprinkle the love potion around a grave at midnight and chant the incantation. Then Madame Lulu says my heart's desire will fall madly in love with me by cock's crow."

"Cockamamy, if you ask me." Linda Sue rolled onto the floor and folded her legs in the lotus position. "Just like your other nutso schemes. Remember when you were going to make a fortune by selling your ant farm's offspring to a gourmet food shop?"

"Yeah. My scaredy-cat big sister left home for a week after she found a crack in my ant nursery."

"And what about when you sent off for all those 'free home trials,' and some humane society sent you a pet python?"

"I'll never forget Petey. Remember how I cried when Adrienne tried to chop his head off with a meat cleaver? Then Mom made me send him back, just because dumb Adrienne has a phobia about animals."

Linda Sue laughed. "You're unreal."

"But I just know my love spell will work." I hugged my pillow, pretending it was Stormy. "What a hunk Stormy is. That gorgeous brown hair, those dreamy eyes, those mus—"

"Baloney. The only real thing about the Garland School's head hunk is that he has a head full of himself."

I shot her a scathing look, like Mom's heroines do in the romance novels she writes. My look fell on Linda Sue's long, reddish blonde hair. I'm secretly jealous of the blondish part. My pixie curls could never be called anything but blackish black.

Linda Sue took a deep breath and touched her forehead to her knees. Talking to her was a lost cause once she started doing yoga. I took my list of potion ingredients out of my desk. I had to find the last two items by midnight tomorrow night. Madame Lulu says March 19 is the Night of the Wishes, when magic spells have the best chance of working. But where in the world would I ever get "a shred of thy love's clothes" and "blood of bat"?

I put a check mark by the "whisker of cat" ingredient, which Linda Sue's Siamese had generously donated. And thanks to Sam's Gourmet Takeout, I checked off "leg of frog."

While Linda Sue maneuvered into another yoga position, I grabbed a chance to talk to her. "Guess what? I found another potion ingredient—smushed slugs."

She gagged, which wasn't surprising with both legs wrapped around her neck. "That is truly gross, Miranda."

"I know. The slugs aren't exactly smushed yet, though."

"How come? You chicken out?" Linda Sue started deep breathing exercises.

"No way. It's just that yesterday I scooped a couple of slugs into a Baggie, and I was all ready to smush them, when paranoid Adrienne came outside armed with insect repellent. She followed me around all day, pestering me to be in the Drama Club skit for the Spring Dance. It's on April first, too. I'd be the April Fools' joke of the school." I shook my head to stop nodding up and down with each inhale and exhale Linda Sue took. "So anyway, I had to stash the slugs in my closet until I could ditch Adrienne. If she finds out about my love spell, she'll give me her boring lecture about fourteen-year-old girls being too young for sixteen-year-old boys."

"What a turkey."

"No kidding. Can you see me in a dance skit? Klutz City. And the way Coach Brody videotapes every single school event, I'd be immortalized as a bozo *on tape*, for pete's sake."

Linda Sue finished her yoga and plopped back on my bed. "Listen, Miranda, I'm not taking Adrienne's side, but I wish you'd give up on Stormy. You're a terrific girl, and he's a loser."

"He is not. And what's so terrific about me? Having well-endowed hips?" I opened my closet and stood sideways looking at myself in the mirror on the door. "I swear, whoever dished out shapes had terrible aim when they got to me."

Linda Sue looked at her own chest. "Join the club."

"Yeah." I shut my closet door and fell across my bed. "Anyway, I can't forget Stormy when my whole entire being is madly in love with him."

"Too bad Stormy Kincaid's whole entire being is madly in love with himself."

"Give me a break. Just because every girl at Garland is dying to date him doesn't make him conceited. Plus, now I have a better chance of getting him to fall for me. Adrienne said Stormy broke up with Julie Phillips."

"Miss Everything? Why would he dump *her*?"

"Easy. I never knew what he saw in her anyway. What does Julie Phillips have that I don't?"

"Try incredible beauty, popularity, wealth."

I socked my pillow. "Oooh, that Julie burns me up. Always bragging about how her mother was a beauty queen, and her father being president of the school board, and her older sisters teaching her tricks to make boys fall for her"

"They must have taught her something, because have you ever seen Julie without a boy around her?" Linda Sue clicked her tongue. "Do I hear a little jealousy on your part, Miranda?"

"Who me? We-ell, maybe a little. I mean, Adrienne doesn't exactly tell me everything I want to know but I am afraid to ask about the dating game. And yesterday I heard Julie bragging about spending a weekend at Hamilton State Teachers

College with her sisters, where she's going to a *fraternity* party, with *college* boys. Why can't Adrienne be like Julie's sisters?"

Linda Sue hopped off my bed. "Oh, who cares about boys anyway? I'm starved. Got any junk food?"

"Food! How can you think of eating when I'm burning my brain over blood of bat and a shred of thy love's clothes?"

"Trust me, Miranda. Even if you dribbled bat's blood hanging nude from the Goodyear blimp, you couldn't get Stormy to notice you. You're just a baby to Mr. Big"

"We'll see." Linda Sue and I headed downstairs, and I heard Mom's typewriter clack from her office in the attic.

"Is your mom writing a new book?" Linda Sue asked.

"Yeah. It's called *Wicked Bliss*."

"Oooh, hot title. What's it about?"

"A French baron who falls in love with an English tutor named Hillary Compton. Mom says the book should be another best-seller, like *Intimate in India*."

Linda Sue sighed as we tromped into the kitchen. "Remember page 49 of that book?"

"Do I ever. Now that's what I need in my life, a page 49."

The phone rang, and I grabbed it. "Hello? . . . Yes, Mrs. Kaminsky, Linda Sue's here."

Linda Sue took the phone. "Hi, Mom. . . . But Mom, I already . . . but I promised Miranda I'd . . ." She replaced the receiver. "Can you believe it? My own mother hung up on me."

"Why? What's wrong?"

"Everything. An important client came into town, and Mom invited her to dinner tomorrow night, with some other people in Mom's law office. She expects me to help."

"Tell her you have to sleep over tomorrow night and that

it's a matter of life and death. Threaten to put arsenic in the hors d'oeuvres if she doesn't let you."

Linda Sue giggled. "I'll give it my best shot. But Mom wants me home *right now*, so I better bail."

She bolted out the kitchen door, and I searched for a snack. Our pantry was in its usual state—empty. The fridge could have passed for a barren wasteland. Only some moldy fruit and congealed leftovers graced its shelves. My stomach growled, and I wished Mom would finish writing *Wicked Bliss* and make her annual pilgrimage to the market.

I pulled out the vegetable drawer. Success! A carton hid inside. I yanked off the lid. Oh, gross. Liver. Worse, it was stale liver. Shriveled gray pieces floated in a bloodbath and smelled like dirty sweat socks. I aimed the carton toward the trash. My arm froze in midtoss.

"Blood!" Blood of liver wasn't "blood of bat," but surely the love spirits would allow one teensy-weensy substitution. I poured some liver blood into a paper cup, then emptied it into my potion jar.

That night I dreamed I'd turned into a shriveled piece of liver. A bat was trying to drink my blood, but there was none left. It was all in a glass jar on my nightstand. The bat raised its claws and shrieked, *"Eieieieieie!"*

I about jumped out of my skin. Then I opened my eyes and realized the shrieking was only my alarm clock. I put on jeans and a sweatshirt and went to wash up. As I headed downstairs, the sound of typing came from the attic.

"Hey, Mom," I called. "I'm meeting Linda Sue at Louisa's Pizza Parlor for lunch. Okay?" Only a rhythmic clickety-clack answered me. I tried again, and I thought she said, "That place is a jungle!" but I couldn't be sure with all that racket going on.

Trails of pipe smoke led me past the den. Dad was hunched over his calculator. It was income tax time, and he'd be incommunicado until he finished figuring his clients' taxes. If I weren't a naturally honest person, I would have asked him for an advance on my allowance. From now until April 15, Dad would agree to anything to get us to leave him alone.

After pedaling uphill to the pizza parlor, my skin crawled with sweat. I wiggled my shirt away from my body to dry off, then went inside. Yummy garlic and cheese smells filtered through the air. I waited for my eyes to adjust to the dimly lit room. Louisa kept it dark so everyone could see the silent movies and "Road Runner" cartoons on the overhead screen. A flickering rainbow of lights shot out of video games lined against one wall, and tables were crowded with people eating pizza. I spotted Linda Sue standing in line.

"No anchovies," I told her, and dug some money out of my pocket. "Here's for my half."

"Thanks." She glanced around the crowded room. "Look, there's some people leaving that booth in the corner. Save us seats, and I'll order the pizza."

"You got it." I skidded across the sawdust floor and fell into the booth, making the soft leather whoosh as I sank into the seat. When Linda Sue scooted in across from me, I told her about finding "blood of bat." "Do you think it will work?"

She shrugged. "Blood by any other name . . ."

"Now all I need is a shred of Stormy's clothes, and my love potion will be complete. Got any ideas?"

"Short of ripping off something from his closet, I give up."

"There has to be a way. If I don't get that last ingredient, Stormy will never fall in love with me. It's not fair. Other girls have boyfriends. What's wrong with me?"

"Nothing besides going after the wrong boy." Linda Sue fiddled with the salt shaker. "I was thinking. If Stormy dumped

Julie, maybe he hasn't asked another girl to the Spring Dance yet. Why don't you ask him to take you?"

"Me? Ask Stormy Kincaid for a date? I couldn't. What if he said no? What if his mother answered the phone?" I squinted at her. "I thought you hated Stormy."

"Hate is a strong word, Miranda. Let's just say I loathe the ground he walks on. But anyway, *you* want a date with him, not me. Maybe Adrienne would ask Stormy for you. Her boyfriend and Stormy are good friends, aren't they? You two could double."

"Are you kidding? Ben is a super guy, but I wouldn't double with Adrienne to a funeral. She'd probably spray the coffin with Lysol. She carries disinfectant around like a security blanket. Adrienne's only allergic to ragweed, but she gets hyper about every little germ."

A 97 flashed on a number board over the pickup counter. While Linda Sue got our order, I glanced around the pizza parlor. Some kids I knew from school were playing video games, and a bunch of children wearing birthday hats were watching "The Little Rascals" on the overhead screen.

A burst of daylight flooded the room as a group of teenagers came in and headed for the pickup line. My breath caught. Standing with the group, in living color, was Stormy Kincaid. Yipes. I couldn't let him see me looking so grubby.

I dashed through the swinging doors to the ladies' room and yanked up my shirt to let the hand dryer blow under my arms. The neon lights over the sink reflected my pale face in the mirror. After brushing my curls, I pinched my cheeks to make them rosy, like Mom's heroines do. My cheeks just looked pinched. Mustering confidence, I charged through the swinging doors.

"Aaah," I cried as a giant pizza tray hit me in the stomach.

Hot tomato sauce splattered on my sweatshirt, and pizza slices fell on the floor. I tripped on one and grabbed the pizza carrier's shirt collar for support. He fell forward, and I ended up dragging him down on top of me.

"My new shirt!" he hollered. "You ripped it."

I blinked, trying to see who was smushing my windpipe. My heart stopped. "Stormy!"

A Shred of Hope

2

"Stormy, I'm sorry I bumped into you," I kept apologizing to him.

"My new shirt's totaled," he moaned. "Uh, but no problem," he said as his friends ran over. "I have others."

Did Stormy realize he still lay on my chest? His closeness was having a fatal effect on my ability to think. When I grabbed his collar, I must have ripped off some buttons on his shirt, because it was open halfway down the front. His tan skin accentuated the hairs on his fantastic, flexing flesh.

Stormy rolled off me and sat up. "Did you see where those buttons went?"

"No, but I'll help you look." I crawled on the floor behind him, sifting sawdust through my fingers and wishing I could think of something clever to say, like Mom's characters do in embarrassing situations.

Stormy sat on his heels. "I give up. A person couldn't find an elephant in this horse feed."

"Want me to keep looking?"

"No thanks. You've done enough already." Stormy glanced at his friends. "That is, I know you didn't mean to ruin my shirt." He took my hand and helped me up. He stood so close I could see whisker stubs on his cheeks. My pulse did jumping jacks.

After what seemed like forever, Stormy backed away. "I better wash the pizza off my shirt," he said.

"Is there anything I can do?"

"No problem. Noooo problem." He backed toward the restrooms, his eyes boring into mine until he disappeared through the swinging doors.

Linda Sue pranced up to me. "Great move, Miranda. The old spill-pizza-on-the-boy's-shirt trick. Gets 'em every time." She laughed. "If Stormy's pals hadn't been around, I bet he'd have used *you* to wipe the stains off his shirt."

"Not true. He was really embarrassed."

"That's my point."

"This isn't an eighth grade crush, Linda Sue. I'm really in love with Stormy. Did you see the way he stared at me, like nobody else mattered?" The vision sent my mind reeling. "I think I mesmerized him. I bet— Ohmigosh. Look!"

"Where?"

"On the floor. It's Stormy's shirt button." I clutched it to my heart. "This button touched Stormy's skin. I'll keep it forever. I'll put it under my pillow at night. I'll . . . Yipes! Do you realize what I'm holding?"

Linda Sue stared at the button. "How many guesses do I get?"

I punched her in the arm. "For your information, this button is 'a shred of thy love's clothes,' one of the potion ingredients I've been looking for. I have to add it to my potion. Want to come with me?"

"In a word, no. But I'm ready to bail. I can't stand cold pizza."

We rode our bikes downhill and stopped at a light on the corner. "What did your mother say about tonight?" I asked her.

Linda Sue sighed. "Still no go."

The thought of exploring a cemetery alone sent a shiver circling my collarbones. "This situation calls for drastic action. Tell your mom if she won't let you sleep over, you'll skip college and live at home forever."

"All riiiight. I'll go for it."

As usual, when we reached Linda Sue's house, I drooled at her pre-Civil War home. What I liked best were the hidden nooks scattered throughout the house. When we were kids, we pretended we were spies for the Underground Railroad and used the nooks for hideouts. We thought the slaves' escape route was really a railroad built underground. I watched her go inside, then coasted the extra block downhill to my house.

I dropped Stormy's button into my potion jar, then crawled into my closet to get the slugs. I reached under the pile of dirty clothes where I'd hidden the Baggie, but all I felt were clothes. I ran through the bathroom between Adrienne's and my room and pounded on her door.

"Did you swipe my slugs?" I hollered.

"I wouldn't take something of yours on a bet," she grumbled, opening the door. "Your room looks like the aftermath of a tornado."

"At least my room doesn't smell like an intensive care unit. I read that disinfectant sprays cause acne."

Adrienne blanched. "Which brands?"

"Brands? Umm, do you use Violet Bouquet?"

She shook her head.

"No? Well how about Satin Sunset?"

Adrienne bolted into the bathroom. Cans clinked in the trash. "Oooh, gross," she hollered. "Miranda, come quick!"

I found her staring into the wastebasket. "My slugs! What were you doing in my closet?" I yanked the Baggie out of the trash.

"Looking for *my* sweater you borrowed. I thought that bag had stale chocolate in it, the way you sneak candy all the time."

"I do not. I've been on the chocolate wagon a whole entire month."

She washed her hands in the sink. "Why were you hiding snails in your closet anyway?"

"None of your business. And they're slugs, not snails. Snails have shells. Don't they teach you anything in tenth grade?"

"Throw those things away. I will not *stand* to have a slug collection in the same house as me."

"I'll help you pack."

"Fun-ny." She marched into her room and slammed the door.

I laughed, then felt my grin freeze on my face. Slimy gunk oozed inside the Baggie. "Oooh, gross out. I smushed the slugs."

After dinner, Adrienne and her boyfriend Ben went to a party, Mom and Dad watched TV, and I kept a low profile in my room. My stomach cramped from hunger. Although Mom had come out of hibernation long enough to bring in Chinese, I couldn't eat a bite. All those egg noodles reminded me of slugs.

Around nine o'clock, I loaded my potion jar, Madame

Lulu's book, and two Snickers I'd hoarded for an emergency into my backpack. A shiver ice-skated up my spine. Linda Sue's mom hadn't budged an inch, and now I had to go to Dreamland Cemetery alone. For security, I tucked the onyx amulet I'd bought at the school charity fair inside my bra. Madame Lulu says onyx is the stone for love.

I giggled, remembering how the owner of the magic charms booth had chased me across the parking lot after his son sold me the amulet. The man probably wanted to up the price from the two dollars I paid. Too bad I gave his son my phone number to call if he got in some bat's blood. He might have given my number to his schizo father.

I flipped through Mom's Russian romance, *Never Say Nyet*. Maybe getting involved in passion would calm my nerves, which were break-dancing throughout my body. After a minute, I shut the book. Even rereading the love scenes Linda Sue and I underlined couldn't squelch the raw fear chipping away at my courage.

At ten o'clock, Mom and Dad came in to say good-night. A little after eleven, I tiptoed down the hall and listened at their door. All was quiet. I slung on my backpack, grabbed my flashlight, and telling myself there were no such things as goblins, ghosts, or ghouls, sneaked outside.

The cold night air hit me like a wallop. I pulled my jacket collar over my ears. The neighborhood houses looked like ominous hulks in the black stillness surrounding me. My imagination ran wild. Branches creaked, and I heard bones breaking. Streetlights shone through the magnolia trees onto the sidewalk, and I saw monster shadows on the pavement. Something skittered under a neighbor's bushes. I hurried up the block.

When I got to Memorial Drive, I slowed down. The street

dead-ended into Dreamland. A padlocked, wrought iron fence enclosed the cemetery. I was shaking all over, but I'd come too far to let fear stop me now. I shinnied up the fence and jumped over, landing on the soggy ground. The cold earth seemed to sink under my fingers. I jerked my hands up and shined my flashlight across the graves.

A sighing wind dusted the grave markers with dry leaves. Large urns, like fat-bellied Buddhas, perched on several tombstones. I forced myself to walk between the graves. According to Madame Lulu's instructions, I had to find a tombstone with an angel on top, then walk thirteen paces north, and stop at the first tombstone I saw without any adornments.

I found an angel, walked thirteen paces, then swept my flashlight over the rows of graves. At the end of the second row to my right, I spotted a square marble slab, large enough to lie down on. It was plain, with no angels or urns on top.

I felt as if a million hollow eyes were watching me as I crept toward the tombstone. In the glow of my flashlight, I read the inscription:

OUR BELOVED SON
MICHAEL OLIVE NEWBERRY
BORN MAY 30, 1940
DIED APRIL 27, 1958

It wasn't hard to figure out that a boy named Michael Olive Newberry died when he was almost eighteen. I wondered how he died so young.

My fingers were stiff, and I could barely open the potion jar. The odor sprang out at me, and I almost dropped the entire potion on Michael Newberry's tombstone. I breathed through my mouth and sprinkled the love potion around his grave.

It was one minute before midnight. I rubbed my amulet between my fingers and chanted the incantation:

> Quintuple, Quadruple, Triple, Double;
> Love potion mix and cauldron bubble.
> Pierce my Stormy's heart with arrows sure;
> Make him desire Miranda with love so pure.
> Oh, spirits of love, hear my plea;
> Make Stormy Kincaid fall in love with me.

I waited for a sign from the love spirits that my spell had worked. I wondered if right this very minute Stormy was tossing in his bed, unable to sleep, his arms aching to hold me, his heart bursting with desire to kiss my lips.

Thunder boomed. Lightning crackled. I fell on the ground and covered my head. A familiar odor rose from the earth. Fright must be warping my senses. The ground smelled like chocolate. Fear giggles escaped my throat. I'd forgotten about the Snickers in my backpack. I probably crushed the candy jumping over the fence.

I peeked through my fingers. Another bolt of lightning zigzagged through the fog which suddenly swirled around the graves.

"L-love sp-spirits?" I stammered. "Is this your s-sign?"

Something rasped.

"P-please don't hurt me," I begged whatever it was. "I'll sp-split right now. I swear."

"No!" a voice roared.

My vital signs ceased.

"Hara-kiri is painful," the voice said. "Not to mention irreversible."

As suddenly as the fog appeared, it lifted, and I felt silly.

A man sat on the tombstone. The voice had come from him. Probably the caretaker. Just my luck to get arrested for disturbing the peace. I shined my flashlight at him to get a better look.

"Hey," I said, "you're no caretaker. You're a boy."

He raised an eyebrow. "How observant."

The boy seemed about Stormy's age, but he definitely lacked Stormy's good taste in grooming. His blond hair was plastered back behind his ears as if he'd matted it down with motor oil. Over a yellowish green shirt, he wore a red cardigan sweater with a navy *G* stitched on the pocket. His baggy slacks barely reached his ankles, revealing blue suede loafers and white socks.

A grin spread across the boy's face. He slid off the tombstone and stretched, making a creaky noise.

Then he walked toward me. An oak tree stood behind the boy's back. The problem was I saw the oak tree *straight through* the boy! I tried to scream, but no sounds came out of my mouth.

He pounded his chest and opened his mouth wide. "Aaauuuurrrgggghhh?"

My heart caved in.

The boy's pale cheeks turned pink. "Excuse me," he said. "But great balls of fire! I've been waiting thirty years to finish that burp!"

A Grave Substitution

3

"W-who? . . . W-who? . . . W-who?" I stammered.

The boy clapped his hands. "Heyyyy. Dig that crazy owl imitation."

I stared at him. Thank goodness nothing icky, like worms or maggots, drooled out of his mouth. And his eyes were pale blue, not hollow sockets. "Are you . . . ?" I nodded toward the tombstone.

"In person."

"But you're s-supposed to be d-dead."

"That's what Charlene Hunnicut thinks, too. She'll blow a gasket when she finds out I've come back."

"Ohmigosh. You really *are* a ghost."

"Heyyyy. We ethereals prefer the term *spirit*. You dig?"

I nodded. My tongue was stuck to the roof of my mouth as if it had been bonded there with Krazy Glue. I estimated the distance to the fence. If I ran fast . . . I took off.

"Hey, don't go." The ghost grabbed me around the waist. I screamed, and he clamped his hand over my mouth. "Promise not to yell if I let you go?"

"Umm. Umm." It was difficult to communicate with his hand making a dental impression in my lips. He let me go and I crumbled on the ground. I rubbed my mouth. My hand smelled like chocolate.

The ghost whipped a comb from his pocket and slicked back his hair. "Don't be afraid. We spirits aren't into torture. A little haunting now and then, but . . ." He spread his arms out, palms up.

I got ready to run if his fingers suddenly grew claws, or his teeth turned into fangs. But he just sat on the ground beside me.

"As I was trying to explain before you went berserk," he said, "I'm here to get revenge on my ex-girlfriend, Charlene. She'll be sorry she cheated on me. That . . . PU! This joint stinks worse than a toad with halitosis."

"Hali-what?"

He narrowed his eyes. "Bad breath."

Hot patches warmed my cheeks. "Oh. You probably smell the love potion I sprinkled around your grave."

"The what around my grave?"

"I didn't hurt your grave. Honest. I wanted to cast a love spell on this guy, but I substituted one of the potion ingredients and . . ."

"Botched the bewitchment, huh?"

"I should have known the love spirits would never go for liver."

"You're darn tootin'. We spirits loathe liver."

"Next time I'll use real bat's blood."

"Heyyyy. You think those spirits had kittens over liver, wait till you hit 'em with bat's blood."

"You don't understand." I told him about Madame Lulu's potion ingredients.

"Your Lulu chick sounds nuttier than a fruitcake. Eyes of

newts and tongues of frogs went out with burying alive."

"So I conjured you by mistake? I mean by substitution?"

"Beats me. All I know is on the Night of the Wishes, if a mortal stands by a spirit's grave at midnight, the spirit gets his wish."

I felt the onyx still in my hand. My love potion might be a dud, but my onyx could really be magic. "So did you wish to get revenge on your ex-girlfriend?" I asked him.

"You bet. I just need to find her. The hussy. Going gaga over that square Floyd Philpotz, and with me barely cold." A purple vein jutted out of his forehead.

I slung on my backpack. "Uh, I have to go now. Good luck finding that girl . . . Charlotte?"

"Charlene. And she's not 'that girl.' Charlene Hunnicut is the most gorgeous chick at the Garland School."

"Garland! I go to Garland."

"No kidding. Maybe you've seen Charlene. Blonde pony-tail, peppermint pedal pushers?"

"Hold it. If Charlene went to Garland with you, that was thirty years ago."

He sighed. "Seems like yesterday. I keep thinking it's still 1958. Boy, am I ever going to get even with her. She actually dropped me for pimple-faced Philpotz. Can you dig it?"

"I can dig it." I'd asked Linda Sue that same question about Stormy falling for Julie Phillips.

"Charlene made her move on Floyd at my funeral," the ghost ranted. "Right in the middle of the minister's eulogy praising how brilliant a student I'd been, how sterling an athlete, how—"

"I get the picture. What I don't get is how you could know Charlene dumped you?"

A pained expression crossed his face. "The spirit lives on, as they say."

"Really? Well, it's been fascinating meeting you, but I've really gotta bail, uh"—I swept my flashlight over his tombstone—"Michael Olive."

"*Olive!*" he roared. "Let me have that flashlight."

I handed it over. I wasn't about to argue with a ghost.

He examined the inscription. "The *r* wore off. My middle name's Oliver. Great balls of fire! You just can't get good cemetery help these days. Hardy har har."

Hardy har har? Was he putting me on?

"My full name is Michael Oliver Newberry, but you can call me by my nickname." He beamed. "It's Monday."

"Where did you get a nickname like that?"

"My initials. M. O. N. stands for Monday. Do you have a nickname, Miranda?"

"Nope. Just . . ." My heart buckled. "How did you know my name?"

"Don't get clutched. I heard your Oscar-winning chant."

"My chant, in case you forgot, is responsible for your being *above*ground."

"You don't know that for sure. Besides, I was never *under*ground."

"Ohmigosh. You were cremated?"

"I've never been cremated in my life. Do you think any sane spirit would spend thirty years *down there*"—Monday nodded toward his grave—"when he could be *up there*"—he gazed at the sky—"enjoying life among the angels?"

He had a point. "Do angels really have halos? What do they do for fun?"

"So many questions. Come on. I'll walk you home."

"Thanks, but I can walk myself home."

"I insist." Monday followed me to the fence. "I hate to ask you this, Miranda, but I don't have anywhere to bunk. How about putting me up at your joint?"

I fell against the fence. "Say what?"

"Just until I find Charlene," Monday said. "You were the mortal standing at my grave at midnight, so you're the only person who can see or hear me."

"I am? Gosh."

"Then you'll let me stay at your place?"

"No. My folks would never go for a spirit in our house. Mom won't even let me have a guppy."

"But you can help me find Charlene. Maybe ask at the school for a forwarding address."

"Are you for real?" I scaled the fence like a squirrel and jumped down to the other side. When Monday didn't follow me, I rested my head between the fence posts to catch my breath.

He kicked the fallen leaves. "Guess I used up my wish for nothing."

Guilt sidled up next to me. Monday was all alone on earth. And here I was probably forcing him to sleep on a park bench with bag ladies and winos. Eeeks. What was I thinking? I'd be a total basket case if a boy stayed at my house. Even a boy ghost.

Monday padded toward his grave. "Well, thanks anyway. See ya later, alligator."

"Uh, bye, Monday. No hard feelings." I pushed away from the fence. My body cooperated, but my head didn't. "Hey, Monday. Wait a minute."

He turned. "Change your mind?"

"Not exactly."

A grin played across his lips.

"It's not funny. These posts are squishing my head."

"I'd like to help, Miranda, but I've gotta scope out a place to bunk. No hard feelings." He walked away.

"Please. I'll do anything if you'll get me loose."

"Anything?" Monday's grin grew wider. "Like in room and board anything?"

I sighed. "You got it."

Monday bent close to me and pressed his palms against my cheeks. I noticed his pale blue eyes had lavender flecks. His hands felt strong, in a gentle sort of way.

"Relax," he said. "I'll have you free in a jif."

"Easy for you to say."

"Ready? One, two, three!" He pushed and I came unstuck.

"Thanks, Monday. You're a wizard." I rubbed my temples. My head had stopped throbbing, if not my nerves. "I, ah, guess we should go to my house now."

"I can dig it. Oops. Wait a sec. I'll be right back."

"Oh, wow!" I said as he disappeared into thin air. "Hey, where'd you go?"

"Here I am." Monday reappeared carrying a large book.

"How did you disappear like that?"

"Sorry. We spirits aren't allowed to tell our secrets. I didn't want to forget my Garland yearbook. Wasn't it neato of my friends to bury it with me?"

"Your friends . . . buried it. . . ." My stomach rolled over. I wanted to ask him how he died, but it seemed too personal a question for a ghost I'd just met.

Monday tucked his yearbook under his arm, and we went to my house. I led him around to the kitchen door. The knob wouldn't budge. "Great. I sneaked out without my key."

"Allow me." He stepped back a few paces, then charged at the door, vanishing through the wood as if it existed only in my imagination.

I felt like one of those cartoon characters whose eyes spring out of their sockets. The door swung open and I went inside.

"That was terrific, Monday. Monday? Hey, where are you?"
I turned on my flashlight and tiptoed into the front hall.

Dad's desk lamp floated across the entry hall. "Heh, heh, heh. Who knows what evil lurks in the hearts of men?"

My skin crawled even though I knew the voice was Monday's. He materialized at my side.

"Aaah," I muffled a scream. "You scared me. I hope you didn't wake my folks."

"I was just playing a little trick, Miranda."

"Very little." I replaced Dad's lamp, then motioned him toward the stairs. He took off. Literally.

"You can fly, too?" I hurried up after him. When I turned on the light in my room, Monday had vanished again.

"Psst. Miranda. Up here." He sailed around the ceiling. "It's a bird, it's a plane, it's . . ."

"Mirrrranda!" Dad's voice boomed from down the hall.

I glared at Monday and opened the door a crack. "Did you call me, Dad?"

"It's after one o'clock in the morning. What are you laughing at?"

"Uh, I was dreaming. It was a comedy."

"So I heard. Go back to sleep and have a nightmare."

"Okay, Dad." I shut the door. "And you, Superman, go find a phone booth and change back into Clark Kent."

"Spoilsport." Monday swooped onto one of my twin beds. "What'll we do now? Want to play checkers?"

"Are you kidding?"

"How about Monopoly?"

"How about sleep?"

"Spirits don't have to sleep. But go ahead. You won't even know I'm here."

"Here?" My heart struck a dissonant chord. Where *does*

one house a ghost? If only we had a guest room. "I've got it. My sister's spending the night at a friend's. Follow me."

Monday glanced around Adrienne's room. "Heyyyy, dig this crazy yellow bedchamber."

"It's called jaundice." I opened a window to let out Adrienne's lilac room deodorant.

"Man, this joint has class." Monday inspected the yellow furniture, yellow print drapes, and yellow flowered wallpaper.

"Makes you want to puke, doesn't it? Listen, please don't mess up in here. My sister has radar like a satellite when it comes to sniffing out filth."

"No sweat." Monday plopped on Adrienne's bed and opened his yearbook.

"Is Charlene's picture in there?" I was falling asleep on my feet, but I was dying to see this girl.

Monday's face lit up like a kleig light. "You betcha. Her mug's plastered all over the place." He flipped to a dog-eared page. A caption read, "Michael Oliver Newberry and Charlene Hunnicut, Spring Dance King and Queen, April 1958."

"Wow, you were Spring Dance King? You must have been popular."

He shrugged. "But isn't Charlene a beaut?"

"Gorgeous," I admitted, sitting on the edge of the bed. Charlene had bangs, and her hair was curled under at the neck, framing her Barbie doll face and toothpaste commercial smile. Personally though, I wouldn't wear such a tacky formal to a Halloween party. Her strapless gown was tight at the waist, and stuck out like porcupine quills down to her ankles. Spiked heels hugged her feet.

"Hey, Monday, you're no slouch in this photo, either." He looked super in a suit, even though his pants were skintight and cut above the ankles. His jacket had narrow lapels, and his tie was thin as spaghetti.

Monday smoothed the fingerprint-smudged page. He'd probably gazed at it a million times. I wondered what Charlene looked like now. I scrutinized her pug nose and rounded chin. She reminded me of someone, but I was too tired to think of whom.

The inscription on Monday's tombstone said he died on April something, 1958, so this photo must have been taken right before he died. I couldn't hold back my curiosity any longer. "I don't mean to pry, Monday, but what happened to you, I mean, how did you . . . ?"

"Die?" He sighed. "I was a counselor at a summer camp. That spring we had a camp reunion at a ski lodge up north. An unpredicted blizzard struck, and one boy got lost. I found him, but by then I couldn't see two inches down the mountain." Monday laughed, but not in a funny way. "The boy made it."

A cold finger poked my heart. Monday had risked his life to save that boy. I wondered if I would have had that much courage. Even though I hardly knew Monday, I couldn't stand to see him so sad. I'd probably regret it, but sometimes I guess a person has to get involved.

I slid off Adrienne's bed. "Monday? I've changed my mind. I'll help you find Charlene."

A House Ghost

4

Daylight slashing through the blinds woke me from the weirdest dream. I was in a cemetery, and this ghost suddenly materialized and asked if he . . .

I bolted out of bed and tapped on Adrienne's door. "Monday? Are you in there?" The only sounds I heard were the *clackety-clack* of Mom's typewriter above, and the *clang-bang* of Dad's pots and pans below. On Sundays he turns into a French chef. I opened the door a crack. Chocolate permeated the air. I never knew room deodorants came in chocolate flavor.

"Good morning, Miranda." Monday floated in through the window.

I leapt a foot off the carpet. "In the future, would you please announce yourself before you scare me into middle age? Where were you?"

"Looking up some old friends. But the only ones I found were Carol Jean Cauthen, Frank Hargrove, and Doug Thornberry." He slumped onto Adrienne's bentwood rocker. "I wish

I had time to look up some of my relatives, but they all live in Texas. And the rules say I have only two weeks to spend on earth. Then I have to go back up there." He nodded toward the sky.

"Two weeks isn't very long." I sat at the foot of Adrienne's bed. "So what was it like to see your friends again?"

"Frustrating. They couldn't see me, and I couldn't even talk to them. Great balls of fire, have they gotten old." He rocked furiously back and forth. "Carol Jean and Frank went steady in high school, and I think they're married now. I was flying over Fifth Street when I saw Frank reading the Sunday paper on somebody's front porch." Monday stopped rocking. "Heyyyy, maybe it was Frank's front porch. Jeepers! Imagine Frank owning his own house. Anyway, Carol Jean came outside and got in a car. She was carrying a briefcase and saying something about calling Frank from New York. Though why she'd be going to New York beats me."

"Maybe on business?" I suggested.

"Naw. Girls don't go on business trips."

"Where have you been? I mean, boy, are you ever in for a surprise."

"Is that so?" Monday started rocking back and forth again, his forehead wrinkled into a frown. In the sunlight, his hair didn't look so greasy. And this teenage ghost didn't have one pimple. Life isn't fair.

"I can't believe Doug Thornberry's got *kids*," Monday said. "He was herding them into a station wagon. The Doug I knew wouldn't be caught dead in any car but a Chevy Impala."

"People change, I guess." I wondered if someday I'd think my high school friends looked old, too. "What about Charlene? Did you go by her house?"

"That was the worst. The joint's deserted, and there's a For Sale sign in the yard. I was going to fly over to my old house, but seeing that sign sort of took the desire away for right now. Maybe tomorrow."

"What a bummer. How about looking up Charlene's or Floyd Philpotz's names in the phone book?"

He snapped his fingers. "Now why didn't I think of that?"

I pulled a phone directory out of my nightstand, and Monday started flipping through the pages the second I gave it to him. But there were no Hunnicuts or Philpotzes listed.

"Where in blazes is Charlene?" he asked.

"Keep the faith, Monday. Somebody will know where to find her."

"How do we find that somebody? Issue an all points bulletin?"

"We don't have to get that drastic. How come you don't know where Charlene is, anyway? I thought spirits could see what happens on earth."

Monday nodded. "We can. I kept the ol' eagle eye on Charlene until her sophomore year at Hamilton State Teachers College. But I came unglued every time I saw her with Floyd. All that kissing just about killed me. So I quit spying on earth."

My heart went out to him. "I know how you feel. If I saw Stormy kiss another girl I'd want to jump in a manhole. But don't worry. Your two weeks are just beginning. We'll find Charlene. In the meantime, I feel grubby from sleeping in my clothes. Do you mind waiting in here while I shower?"

"Sure. No sweat." He sighed. "Aaah, a real shower. Miranda, could I ask you a teensy-weensy favor?"

"What?" I didn't know if I wanted to hear this.

"The thing is, we spirits don't have to bathe, but it *has* been thirty years and—"

"Thirty years! Gross."

"I want to see if a hot shower still feels good. So could I take one after you finish?"

"Sounds reasonable. Just don't stay in the shower all day. My dad is a demon when it comes to the water bill."

"I can dig it." Monday kicked off his shoes. Clods of dirt fell on Adrienne's carpet.

I gasped. *Grave dirt*. "Don't move. I'll be right back." I ran down the hall for the vacuum and rolled it into Adrienne's room. "Here. You spilled, you clean."

"Are you kidding? I don't do dames' work."

"That does it. I let you get by with saying girls don't take business trips, but now you've gone too far. It just so happens we *dames* have made a few advances in the past thirty years. Ever hear of women's lib?"

"Who?"

"Women's rights. In a nutshell, girls can do anything boys can these days. So plug in the cord and push."

Monday looked at the vacuum cleaner as if it might bite him. "We-ell, I guess once won't hurt."

"Sport." I made sure he cleaned up every speck. All I needed was for Adrienne to find dirt on her carpet. Plus, if anyone came in, I could grab the vacuum so they wouldn't think it was running by itself.

When Monday finished, I took a shower and put on a pair of navy Bermudas and my T-shirt that said Teenager Is Not a Dirty Word. When I went back into Adrienne's room, Monday was looking through his yearbook.

"Heyyyy," he said, staring at me. "Those are hip shorts."

"Thanks, but don't mention hips. I gave up chocolate because of mine."

"Chocolate." Monday drooled. "I could die for chocolate."

I was tempted to tell him it was too late for that.

"We spirits don't have to eat, but I never lost my craving for chocolate. Guess you could call me a chocoholic spirit."

Just my luck to conjure a chocolate-loving ghost. "Well, Monday, being the generous martyr that I am, I'll give you a treat." I dug out the Snickers I'd stashed in my backpack. They weren't smushed like I thought.

Monday wolfed down one Snickers while he peeled the wrapper off the second. "Umm-umm good. Thanks, Miranda. These are lifesavers."

"No they're not. They're Snickers. Hardy har har."

He groaned. "Next time, though, could you get me Hershey's Kisses? They're my favorite. I was going nuts for one last night."

Last night. The chocolate smell at the cemetery I thought was my Snickers, and the odor in Adrienne's room I thought was chocolate deodorant. "Uh, Monday, have you noticed you smell? Not a bad smell. What I mean is, do you have some kind of chocolate odor?"

He grinned. "I wondered when you'd notice. I've given off that scent since I got up there. Maybe it's a way of giving us spirits our favorite food on earth, to make us feel at home, so to speak."

"Does everyone up there smell like you?"

"Great balls of fire! If all spirits smelled like chocolate, I'd be in the angelic loony bin."

I was on a roll. If I played my cards right, maybe he'd tell me more about what up there was really like. "Uh, Monday, do all spirits have your fantastic taste in clothes?"

He wiped his knuckles across his sweater. "Aren't these duds the most?"

"Totally." If you liked baggy pants and loud shirts.

"We spirits usually stay dressed in the clothes we left earth in. But heyyyy. I wasn't called the leader of the pack in high school for nothing. I was the first guy in my class to wear chartreuse shirts."

"I bet you knocked everyone out." Or blinded them. That glaring yellow-green could light up Milwaukee. "So what do you spirits do all day?"

"Lots of things. Did I mention I'm captain of the Angels baseball team? Then there's cloud surfing, and . . . Oh no you don't. You're trying to trick me into blabbing about life up there. You can save your breath, because I'm hitting the shower. See ya later, alligator." He charged through the bathroom door without bothering to open it.

"That trick is getting so old," I called after him.

While Monday showered, I phoned Linda Sue. Her line was busy. If her mom was talking, I'd never get through. Mrs. Kaminsky was a committee person like Adrienne, always yakking with her volunteers. But I had to give Adrienne credit for coming up with a theme for this year's Spring Dance. Since the dance was also the thirtieth reunion for the class of '58, Adrienne suggested doing everything in a fifties motif. Fifties, 1958. That was *thirty years ago!* Boy was I dense. Now I knew where Monday would find Charlene. Surely she'd show up at her own class reunion.

I tapped on the bathroom door. "Monday, hurry up. I have something important to tell you."

"Almost done," he called.

"Well, it's about—"

"Who's been sleeping in my bed?" Adrienne growled, bursting into my room from the hall.

"Who are *you* supposed to be?" I growled back. "Papa Bear?"

She glared at me. "My bedspread is wrinkled, and my room smells like a crypt."

My heart lurched. I moved in front of the bathroom door.

Adrienne's eagle eyes didn't miss a trick. "Why is the shower running in there?" she demanded. "And why is the bathroom door locked from my bedroom?"

"I locked the door because I'm, uh, I'm steaming my jeans."

"Hey, Miranda," Monday called. "Got any Brylcreem on ya?"

"Shhh." I pressed against the door.

"Who're you telling to shush?" Adrienne asked.

"N-nobody. I was practicing my whistle. Ssss, ssss. See?"

She looked doubtful and headed for my closet. "I need my rust skirt you borrowed last week."

"Be my guest. I only wore your dorky old skirt because Mom wanted me to look nice when her editor came to dinner."

"You couldn't look nice if you were outfitted by Calvin Klein himself." Adrienne disappeared into my closet. "This is disgusting, Miranda. I can't find a thing with all your junk in here."

Hangers clanged and boxes shuffled across the floor. My closet sounded as if it housed a poltergeist.

Monday opened the bathroom door a crack. "What about that Brylcreem? My ducks won't do a thing without it."

"Ducks?" I whispered. Thank goodness Adrienne was making such a racket she couldn't hear me. "Do you have a duck in there?" I asked Monday. "I told you my mom doesn't allow pets."

"Tell me the truth, Miranda. Are we really in America, or did I miscalculate and materialize on Mars? No offense, but you'd have more luck with this Stormy guy if you knew what's cool these days."

"I'm not believing this."

"Don't be embarrassed. I'll clue you in." He leaned the back of his head out the door and smoothed his hair to a point at the nape of his neck. "This is called ducks, because my hair looks like a duck's tail. Brylcreem makes it stay in place. You know, 'Brylcreem,' " he sang, " 'a little dab'll do ya.' "

"Cute. Is that what makes your hair so greas . . . so smooth?"

"You betcha."

Adrienne clomped out of my closet carrying her skirt. I slammed the bathroom door shut. "Just checking on my jeans. Don't go in there," I said as she started toward me. "It's really steamy, and your hair will frizz."

Adrienne frowned, then headed for the hall door. "Actually, Miranda," she said, "you looked good in this skirt. Maybe you should wear rust more often." She patted my head and left.

Go figure big sisters. One minute they put you down, and the next they offer to color coordinate you.

Monday materialized looking squeaky clean and smelling like Godiva chocolate. I drooled, but not because of his odor. In spite of the fact that he was a ghost, plus old enough to be my father if you counted grave time, Michael Oliver Newberry was a hunk.

The phone rang. I grabbed it, hoping the caller was Linda Sue.

"Miranda Taylor please," a man said.

My pulse went into suspended animation. What if someone saw me sneak into Dreamland? "This is Miranda," I finally admitted.

"Edward Ogelthorpe here. I'll get right to the point. Did you buy an onyx amulet at the Garland School's charity fair?"

The man was CIA or FBI for sure. Cops always read you your rights before asking questions. Was breaking and entering a cemetery a misdemeanor or a felony? Yipes. I could end up graduating high school in jail.

"Well, did you buy that onyx amulet?" Mr. Ogelthorpe asked.

"Guilty as charged." Might as well confess. He probably had the goods on me anyway.

"Miss Taylor, there has been a dreadful mistake. I must have that amulet back immediately."

A Philpotz
by Any Other Name

5

I almost dropped the phone. "Why should I give you back the amulet?" I asked. "I didn't steal it."

"I didn't say you lifted, uh, stole the onyx." The man's voice squeaked like an out-of-tune violin. "The fact is my son Harold sold you that amulet by mistake. That stone has been in my family for generations."

"You mean it's a family heirloom?"

"Heirloom? Ah, yes. I would have called you sooner, but Harold misplaced your phone number. I just found it behind the voodoo dolls."

"The voodoo dolls! Okay, Linda Sue. The joke's up. I know this is you. You're just disguising your voice."

"I am not. Now see here . . ."

"Oh, I get it. You're a boy Linda Sue got to play a trick on me. Okay, whoever you are, let me talk to Linda Sue."

"This is no joke. Just return the amulet, and I'll give you another."

"In a pig's eye." Two could play Linda Sue's game.

"Listen, missy, I want that onyx back. That is, the stone's

value is purely sentimental. I'll give you something else in exchange."

"Hmmm. Got any bat's blood on you?"

"Look here, kid. . . ."

"No bat's blood, no deal."

A sigh blew through the receiver. "Very well. Come to my booth during the swap meet next Saturday at Hamilton College Stadium. I might have some bat's blood." The phone clicked.

I stared at the receiver. "Monday, can you believe Linda Sue? Joking around when . . . Monday? Aw, give me a break. Don't you play tricks on me, too." I peeked under my beds and in my closet.

Yummy bacon smells wafted up from the kitchen. "Okay, be that way. I'm going downstairs to eat, and we're having Hershey's Kisses for dessert." No Monday. If mentioning chocolate didn't make him materialize, he must have bailed. But where did he go?

After brunch, Monday still hadn't returned. I tried to study for an algebra quiz, but thoughts of Monday kept creeping into my brain.

The next morning, I woke up in a mood somewhere between high anxiety and intense irritation. The nerve of that ghost, butting into my life, then butting out again without so much as a "See ya later, alligator." Plus he'd made me so nervous I couldn't study for my algebra quiz. Maybe my amulet would help me pass. I'd take it to school and rub it right before Ms. Dunnahoo handed out the tests.

I took a quick shower, scarfed down a granola bar, and ran to catch the school bus. I didn't see Linda Sue until lunch.

She waved from the end of a crowded cafeteria table. "Hurry, Miranda. I saved us seats."

"Be right there." The instant I passed the steam trays, greasy smells of selected Salmonella almost made me puke. I bought cottage cheese and milk, then weaved my way between the lunch tables to Linda Sue.

She banged her milk carton down. "How come you never called me yesterday? I sat by the phone practically all day."

"*Me* phone *you*?" I sat between Linda Sue and another girl who was eating a sandwich while reading a history book. "How come you had a boy phone me pretending to be some Ogelthorpe?"

"What's an Ogelthorpe?" she asked.

"Not a what, a who." I repeated my conversation with the alleged Mr. Ogelthorpe.

"Read my lips, Miranda. I did not play a phone prank on you."

I sort of believed her. "Okay, let's drop it. Anyway, I'm dying to tell you what happened at Dreamland."

She choked on an Oreo. "You went?" she gasped after chugging some milk. "What happened? Tell, tell."

I did. "Oh, I wish you could see Monday. He's so handsome. Hey, what are you laughing at?"

"That name. Monday? Really, Miranda. Couldn't you come up with something a little more dazzling?"

"You wouldn't laugh if you saw him. He has these gorgeous, pale blue eyes, and blond hair, and he's . . ."

"Invisible to everyone but you, right?"

"How'd you know?"

"Lucky guess." She glanced over her shoulder. "Is he, uh, here now?"

"You don't believe me." I gouged open my milk carton, and a splat of milk hit my nose. "Figures. My whole entire love life is going down the tubes, and now my best friend thinks I'm a mental case."

"I do not. I just meant you *are* a bit old to have an invisible friend."

"He's not invisible! I mean, he's invisible right now because he isn't here right now. But when Monday comes back, he'll materialize and I'll see him perfectly."

"Relief to the max."

"I can't believe you're making jokes when I'm going crazy worrying about Monday. What if he's lost? It's been thirty years since he roamed the neighborhood."

Linda Sue raised her eyebrows, and the freckles on her forehead hid between the wrinkle lines. "Keep the faith, Miranda. Your invisible friend will return someday. Tinkerbell did. Just clap your hands and say, 'I believe in fairies. I believe in fairies.' "

I glared at her.

"It's a free country," she said in a baby voice. "And if I don't wanna believe in ghosts, you can't make me." She blew up her empty Oreo bag and popped it.

I jumped out of my seat.

"Sorry," she said. "Anyway, here's a question for you. Suppose Monday *is* real. How come right away you claim he's a friendly ghost? You've known Stormy since the sixth grade, and you've never once said he was friendly."

"For pete's sake, Linda Sue. I've told you a jillion times how handsome Stormy is, and what a super baseball pitcher he is, and how he always makes straight A's."

"That's superficial stuff. I meant how he treats you, which, if you ask me, is like you were a wart on his nose."

Loud laughter wiped out my comeback. I looked for the source, and my mouth went dry. It was Stormy. A bunch of beautiful girls swarmed around him. I ducked under the table. "Psst. Linda Sue, look at me. Do I need lipstick? Is there food stuck between my teeth?"

"Will you get out from under that table? With all those girls around him, Stormy can't see you anyway." She looked at Stormy and rolled her eyes. "Toss my dirty tray for me, okay? I have to study for a Spanish test next period." She hurried out of the cafeteria.

Uh-oh. My algebra test was after study hall. I peeked at Stormy on my way to the used tray racks. He smiled, and I almost fell down. Stormy Kincaid actually smiled at me. I couldn't wait to find some real bat's blood and cast my love spell again. This afternoon, I'd put an ad for bat's blood in the neighborhood classifieds.

But right now I needed to concentrate on my amulet and the algebra test. I reached inside my purse for the onyx. Oh, no. It wasn't there. I must have been thinking so hard about where Monday was that I forgot to put it in my purse.

I ran to study hall before the bell rang and started cramming. When Ms. Dunnahoo handed out the algebra tests, I wanted to kick myself again for leaving the onyx at home. The problems were super hard. I was still kicking myself when Linda Sue and I met at our lockers after school. I told her about the amulet.

"Why are you so into magic all of a sudden?" she asked. "First you believe a ghost followed you home Saturday night, and now you're counting on a rock to make you pass a test."

I banged open my locker. "But my amulet helped me conjure Monday."

"That remains to be seen." She took some books out of her locker. "By the way, any word from the 'Twilight Zone'? Doot-do-doot-do, doot-do-doot-do," she sang the show's theme song.

"No, and I'm really worried."

"Maybe your ghost went looking for his girlfriend."

"*Ex*-girlfriend." I dug through mountains of wadded-up paper and stale candy wrappers until I found the books I needed to take home. "Boy, Charlene Hunnicut sure reminds me of someone. It's killing me trying to think who she— Help!" My legs whipped out from under me. But I didn't fall. I floated.

"Miranda!" Linda Sue yelled. "You're flying."

My body zoomed forward, and kids pointed at me, their mouths gaping. Linda Sue caught up to me just as something bumped into my nose. I stared into a pair of pale blue eyes.

Monday grinned. "Good afternoon, Miranda."

"Where have you been?" My voice sounded bumpy as he bounced me in his arms.

"I was taking care of a little *spiritual* business." Monday ran down the stairs to the first floor.

Linda Sue kept up the pace. "Miranda, is it h-him?"

My head bobbed up and down without my moving a muscle.

Monday burst into the attendance office. The secretary, Miss Klopnast, jumped about three feet off her chair, knocking over a bottle of red fingernail polish. Monday set me on my feet, and I fell against the counter separating the office staff from the waiting area.

"Look what you did," I griped at him.

"Me!" Miss Klopnast bellowed. "You're the one who bombed in here like a bat outta . . . like a hurricane."

Linda Sue stumbled in chanting, "I do believe in ghosts, I do believe in ghosts." She dropped my books in a heap by the door.

"Hey, thanks," I said as she doubled over. "I would have been dead without those books."

Miss Klopnast sneered. "I wouldn't press my luck, dearie."

Monday nudged me. "Ask her about Charlene. Hurry up."

"Okay. Okay. Uh, Miss Klopnast, I know this will sound weird, but do you have a forwarding address for a Charlene Hunnicut who graduated from Garland in 1958?"

She snorted like a warthog. "Listen, dearie, at Garland, we just educate 'em and graduate 'em. After that, out with the old, in with the new."

Monday's face drooped.

Linda Sue edged up to me. "We better jam, Miranda. If Klopnast blabs to Smedley . . ."

As if on cue, the principal flung open the door to his private office. He led a fat, balding man out with him. Mr. Smedley shook the man's hand. "Glad you dropped by, Mr. Phillips."

Linda Sue poked me. "Phillips as in Julie Phillips?"

I shrugged.

Mr. Phillips pumped the principal's hand. "I'm sure the Spring Dance will be a memorable occasion, Smedley. About time Garland honored my class."

Mr. Smedley nodded. "Oh, I almost forgot. Remember your old principal, Mr. Alexander? He's in a nursing home now. Such a shame. But he's videotaping a speech to be shown the night of the dance."

Mr. Phillips wiped his flabby cheeks with a handkerchief. "Capital, Smedley. And I know my wife will be tickled pink when she hears the school is commemorating her reign as queen."

I motioned Monday toward the door, but he was staring at Mr. Phillips as if he were a deadly virus.

"So it's *Phillips* now, is it?" Monday said. "Well, you can change your last name a thousand times for all I care. But you're still the low-life cube who stole my girl, Mister Floyd Philpotz."

Taken for a Ride

6

"Floyd Phillips is Philpotz?" I blurted.

Miss Klopnast frowned, and I tried to blend into the wall. Linda Sue crouched behind me. "What's Monday doing?"

"I think he's strangling Philpotz."

Monday had Mr. Phillips in a judo hold around his neck. "Tell me the truth, Philpotz," he said. "Did you marry Charlene?"

"Help," Mr. Phillips said, choking. "I can't breathe."

Miss Klopnast wrung her hands. "Mr. Smedley, *do* something. You're the principal."

Mr. Smedley inched up to Mr. Phillips. "Are you choking, Phillips?"

"Aaaggghhh," he rasped.

Monday grabbed Mr. Phillips's arms and shook him. Mr. Phillips vibrated like he'd been struck with a tuning fork. "Answer me, or I'll have to get rough with you. Where is she?"

If this was Monday being gentle, I dreaded seeing him get

rough. I kicked his shin. He hollered and rubbed his leg. Mr. Phillips dropped to his knees, his body so stiff I thought rigor mortis had set in.

Mr. Smedley ran toward the door. "I'll get the nurse."

Monday raised his fist. "Lemme at him. Lemme at him."

Mr. Phillips gasped. "Did you catch him?"

"Who?" Miss Klopnast asked.

"The person who tried to strangle me."

"Nobody was here but us," she insisted.

Mr. Phillips glanced around. "Then it had to be a . . . a poltergeist."

Monday laughed. "Close."

Mr. Phillips struggled to his feet. "Miss Klopnast, I want this office bugged immediately for evidence of extrasensory phenomena. Understand?"

She backed up to her desk. "I'll write a memo."

Mr. Phillips waddled out the door and Linda Sue moved out from behind me. "That man is a bigger bozo than his daughter," she said.

"Julie? That good old girl who loves all males, whether punk, hunk, or funk? Ohmigosh. That's who Charlene reminds me of. Hamilton State Teachers College. I should have guessed." I grabbed my books and dashed out the door.

Monday flew after me. "Heyyyy, where are you going?"

"To Julie's house to find Charlene . . . I hope."

"Miranda, wait up," Linda Sue hollered.

I bolted outside and thought I'd accidentally stumbled into a furnace. The temperature must have gone up ninety degrees since this morning. I'd been sweltering during last period, but I thought it was from the formaldehyde odor that's always stinking up my biology lab.

I forced myself to keep running through the heat, and I was almost at the bus stop when a bus swung away from the curb. I shouted at the driver to stop. A cloud of exhaust spewed out of the tailpipe in response.

"You crumb," Linda Sue shouted, catching up to me.

Monday thudded to a landing at the corner. "Drat it. How long before the next bus?"

"At least twenty minutes," I told him.

He stared at a 7-Eleven store across the street. "How about buying me those Hershey's Kisses you promised?"

I put my books on the bus stop bench. Maybe the 7-Eleven had their air-conditioning turned on. "Okay," I told Monday. "But stay here. I'm fresh out of spirit excuses."

"Scout's honor," he promised. "I'll behave."

Linda Sue's eyes sparkled when I told her what Monday wanted. "Junk food. Super idea." She flung her books on top of mine.

We crossed the street and went inside the market. Aaah. It was like walking into an igloo. Linda Sue headed up an aisle marked Cookies, Chips, Gum, and I angled toward the cashier, a middle-aged woman with peppery hair.

"Excuse me, ma'am," I said, "but do you have Hershey's Kisses?"

"Aisle four," she answered, ringing up a six-pack of soda for a boy with wavy brown hair, a great build, and . . . Ohmigosh. It was Stormy.

I twisted into a hairpin turn, right into a rack of batteries. They hit the floor and rolled in all directions, including under Stormy's feet. He tripped and the six-pack fell on his foot.

"Owowow!" He hopped up and down, holding his foot.

I cringed. This made the second time I'd klutzed out in front of him. "Are you okay? Is anything broken?"

"F-fine. I'm fine." He stopped hopping and picked up the six-pack.

Linda Sue appeared from behind the cookie aisle carrying

a package of cupcakes. "Miranda, why are you on the floor?" She noticed Stormy. "Never mind. I can guess."

"It was an accident, Linda Sue." Trying to act casual, I crawled around picking up the batteries, as if demolishing a 7-Eleven were an everyday occurrence.

"Need some help with those batteries?" Stormy asked, backing toward the exit.

"Oh, no thanks. I've got everything under control. Need any help with those sodas?"

"No way. I mean, I can handle it." He opened the door and limped out.

Why was I so clumsy around him? At this rate, before I could cast my love spell again he'd be in a body cast.

Linda Sue and I paid for our snacks and made it back across the street just as a bus pulled to the curb. We grabbed our books and leapt on. I sneaked Monday his chocolate, and by the time we reached Mulberry Avenue, Julie's street, he'd scarfed the whole bag. I was surprised he could even get off the ground to fly the three blocks uphill to Julie's house.

"Heyyyy, where is this joint?" Monday asked as we turned into a long, winding driveway.

"We have to get through the Enchanted Forest first," I told him.

More than a hundred mulberry trees, their branches dripping purplish red berries, lined the Phillips's driveway. We emerged onto a sloping lawn. The lush green was interrupted sporadically by exotic flower gardens carved into the grass. I grinned at the stunned expression on Monday's face.

"Holy moly," he exclaimed. "Dig this pad."

I laughed. "Julie calls it Mulberry Estates."

Her Victorian mansion, complete with widow's walk rimming three sides of the third story, looked like it had waltzed straight off the pages of a Charlotte Brontë novel.

Linda Sue and I climbed the steps to the front porch spanning the width of the house. A breeze swept across the porch, and I was tempted to plop on one of the wicker chaises with their fluffy print cushions. Monday hesitated before stepping onto the porch.

"What's the matter?" I asked him. "I thought you wanted to find out if Charlene lives here."

"I'm kinda nervous," he said. "It's been thirty years since I've seen her, you know."

"Don't worry," Linda Sue said when I told her about Monday's nerves. She spoke toward a spot above my right shoulder. "Charlene can't see you anyway."

Monday slapped his forehead. "Right. I keep forgetting I'm not a mortal."

I put my books on the porch and knocked on the door.

In a few seconds, Julie opened the door. "Hiiii. . . . Oh, it's you. I was expecting Stormy. He's coming over to swim."

Monday gasped. "Charlene! What happened to you? Where's your ponytail?"

"Hi, *Julie*," I said, hoping Monday would catch on that this girl wasn't Charlene.

He stared hard at Julie.

She wore a skimpy bikini on her body and a grimace on her face, as if Linda Sue and I were bags of garbage someone had dumped on her doorstep. She flipped her chestnut-colored hair over one shoulder.

I wanted to explode. Why did Julie's hair fluff while my short curls frizzed like I was a Siamese twin to an electric socket? (Linda Sue tried ironing my curls once. The iron straightened my hair, right onto the floor, and I almost ended up with a Mohawk.)

Julie smeared suntan oil on her arms. "So why'd you come over?"

I glanced at Monday. He stood stiffly, as if he'd taken a bath in starch. I cleared my throat. "Uh, we heard about your mother being honored at the Spring Dance, and we wanted to see if she was Char . . . uh, we wanted to talk to her."

"About what?"

"Umm, about . . ."

"An article," Linda Sue piped up. "For the *Garland Gazette*."

Julie squealed. "My mom in the school paper? Far out."

"Isn't it?" Linda Sue put her books next to mine and took a notepad and pencil from her purse. "We thought the title could go something like, 'After Thirty Years, Former Beauty Queen Still Going Strong.' "

"Awesome." Julie sank onto one of the chaises. "Mom was the most beautiful girl at the Garland School. Everyone says I look just like her."

"How modest," I said and sat on a chaise, too. "So can we talk to her?"

"Oh no," Julie said. "Mom's at Le Germaine Beauty Spa getting in shape for the Spring Dance. She won't be back until that Friday. But"—slowly her frown disintegrated into a cagey grin—"I know everything about my mother. You could interview *me* about *her*."

"Wonderful." Linda Sue plopped on the third chaise. "Okay, Julie. Shoot."

Julie jumped up. "Wait a sec. My cheerleading pictures just came back. You could use some in the article."

"Another time," Linda Sue said, fanning herself with her notepad. "We're here to write about your mother."

Julie's face scrunched into a pout. She sat down again.

"Just the facts, ma'am," Monday said and flew to sit on a tree branch at the side of the porch.

"Facts," I repeated. "Like what was your mother's maiden name?"

Monday leaned far out from the branch, his eyes wide.

"Hunnicut," Julie answered.

Monday fell out of the tree. "So! That two-timing hussy *did* marry Philpotz."

Linda Sue tapped her pencil. "Now, Julie, our readers want to know the private poop. Like who were your mom's boyfriends in high school, how she met your father, when they got married. Got any tidbits along those lines you'd care to impart?"

Julie's amber eyes glittered. "We-ell, Mother did have one steady boyfriend before Dad. Michael something."

Linda Sue leaned closer to Julie. "What happened to this Michael?"

"A terrible tragedy." Julie lifted her leg and rubbed suntan oil on her thigh. "The boy died. Mother about fell apart."

Monday snorted. "Yeah, she ate her heart out."

"But Daddy convinced Mom not to grieve her life away," Julie went on. " 'Charlene,' Daddy said, 'you're worth much more than that hood.' "

I gasped. "What a creep."

Julie nodded. "That's what Daddy called him, too."

Linda Sue scribbled furiously on her notepad.

Monday's face blistered. "I should have finished off *Daddy* this afternoon."

Julie raised her bikini bottom a tiny bit over her hip and stared at her leg. "Look, I'm getting tan already. See my tan line?"

"That's nice," Linda Sue said. "But you were talking about your mom and dad. What happened next?"

"Oh yeah. Well, after that boy died, Mom went to Hamilton

State Teachers College. That's where my sisters go now. Anyway, the summer after Mom's sophomore year, Daddy insisted that she marry him. He said, 'Charlene, why do you need to teach school when you could be my wife and not trouble your pretty little mind about a job? You can marry me and just take care of our house and raise our kids.' Wasn't that romantic?"

Chauvinistic was more like it. "It takes all kinds," I said.

Monday shook his fists. "If Floyd were here right now, I'd, I'd . . ."

Julie sighed. "So Mom and Dad got married that Christmas. And then they had Joan and Jan."

Linda Sue stopped taking notes. "Joan, Jan, and Julie? You could have been the Pointer Sisters."

"Not really. I can't carry a tune. Did I tell you I was born five years after Jan?"

The phone rang, and Julie ran inside to answer it. I was tempted to go jump in her pool, but in about a minute, she bounded back outside. "Great news. Guess who was elected Spring Dance Queen this year?"

Linda Sue rubbed her chin. "Miss Piggy?"

"No, silly. Me! Stormy's the King."

"He sure is," I said.

Julie patted my arm. "You have a crush on Stormy, don't you? I bet after he and I had that fight, you hoped he'd ask you out." She swiveled her hips and did a model's walk back to the chaise she'd been sitting on. "What you don't understand, Miranda, is that what Stormy and I have is true love, while what you feel for him is only puppy love." She flipped her hair over one shoulder. "A silly argument will never break Stormy and me up for good."

"You're all heart," I told her.

"Is there anything else I can tell you about Mom?" she asked. "I need time to fix my makeup before Stormy gets here."

"I hope he's not due for about five hours," I said. "So you'll have enough time."

Monday laughed. "That's telling her."

Julie opened her mouth, then shut it and strutted toward her front door.

I itched to get even with her, and all of a sudden, without even thinking, I said, "Wait a minute, Julie. I just remembered that we saw Stormy at the 7-Eleven before we came over, and I could swear he mentioned being in a hurry to pick up Judy Enders. Something about a victory celebration. Maybe for being elected Spring Dance King?"

Linda Sue frowned, then grinned. "Oh yeahhhh. You mean Stormy didn't invite *you*, Julie?"

I patted her arm. "But Stormy could have said *Julie*, instead of *Judy*. There was lots of noise in the store at the time."

"Well!" Julie huffed. "As far as I'm concerned, Mr. Kincaid can just find himself another swimming pool to use. Mine just closed for the season." She started inside. "I'm going to phone Stormy right now to tell him off."

"Right on," I said, unable to stop the smile rushing across my lips. I don't usually lie, but whoever said, "Don't get mad. Get even," sure knew what he was talking about.

"Thanks for telling me about Stormy," Julie said. "I owe you."

"Oh, it was nothing, Julie." I bit the inside of my cheek to keep from laughing.

"We better go," Linda Sue said.

"Later, Julie." I picked up my books and started down her front lawn.

"Yeah, later," Monday echoed. "See ya later, alligator."

At the bus stop, I finally let myself laugh out loud. Linda Sue giggled so hard she fell down.

"Monday," I said when I stopped laughing. "When do you want to come back and get your revenge on Charlene?"

"I'm not going to get even with Charlene here." He rubbed his hands. "Old Floyd himself gave me the idea. And I know the perfect place to get revenge on Miss Charlene Hunnicut Philpotz Phillips."

Toad-ally Cut Up

7

The next day was a little cooler, and the weatherman promised the temperature would continue its downswing. I hoped he was right, because the Spring Dance would be held in the gym, which wasn't air-conditioned.

While I was at school, Monday went to look up some more of his high school friends. At lunch I was wondering if he'd had any luck, when Julie Phillips charged up to me in the cafeteria line and chewed me out. She'd phoned Stormy to let him have it for taking out another girl. He'd denied even knowing a Judy Enders, and had broken their date for the Spring Dance. Hot dog! Then I felt guilty for playing a trick on Julie, until she swore she'd get Stormy back anyway, and I knew she probably would. I decided to keep looking for bat's blood so I could cast another love spell.

The good news was last night I did some serious studying for another algebra test, and I remembered to bring my amulet to school today. I knew my amulet was magic the minute Ms. Dunnahoo handed out the tests. The algebra problems were cinchy. I'd probably get at least a B, and that would make up for the D I'd gotten on yesterday's quiz, when I forgot to bring my amulet.

I was in such a good mood, I actually smiled going into biology lab last period, my least favorite class. I fell into my seat behind one of the long work tables. My good mood didn't last long, though, because as usual, the putrid odor of formaldehyde made me queasy.

Mr. Bunyon, my science teacher, scribbled an assignment on the board. He was short with a Santa Claus belly and stood bent forward, like the Leaning Tower of Pisa. Whenever I saw him, I had this crazy urge to punch him over and see if he'd pop back up like one of those inflatable clowns.

As the rest of the class straggled in, I copied the homework assignment in my notebook, then read what today's lab project was, which Mr. Bunyon had scrawled in his usual corny way: *Go directly to your table, do not pass Go, but do collect your . . .*

"FROGS!" I yelled. "We're going to cut up frogs?"

Mr. Bunyon looked as if I'd thrown a tomato at him. "This is not home ec, Miss Taylor. We don't *cut up* in here. We *dissect*."

Some kids snickered. Dissect, shmisect, as Linda Sue would say. We were still going to slice up a toad. Caroline, the girl who sat behind me, looked like she was in ecstasy.

"Awesome," she said. "Our first live specimen."

Larry, a real class clown, clutched his throat. "Frogs! We'll all get warts."

Mr. Bunyon scowled. "That's a myth. Furthermore, these frogs are not alive. I pithed them myself."

I leaned toward the boy who sat next to me. "Joey, what does pith mean?"

"Kizzzttt." He drew his finger across his neck.

"That's criminal. Someone ought to inform the SPCA."

He laughed. "Now, Miranda, don't rush out and form a committee to save the frog. Those toads don't feel a thing. One bang on the head, and kizzzttt."

"I think I'm gonna be sick."

Mr. Bunyon glared us into silence and handed out frog specimens in individual trays. The class grew so quiet I could hear Mrs. Hernandez conjugating Spanish verbs two doors down. For once, even Larry didn't mouth off.

"Consider yourselves fortunate to have your own specimens," Mr. Bunyon said. "After spring vacation, Garland will enroll several new students from McKinley High." He clicked his tongue. "McKinley's the second school in our area this year forced to close for lack of funds. At any rate, you students will soon have to share specimens."

Good. I'd let my lab partner do the dirty work. I giggled inside, then gulped. Another odor had come into the room. Chocolate.

"Greetings, Miranda." Monday materialized in the empty seat to my right.

I jumped. "What are you doing here?"

Mr. Bunyon stopped dealing out frogs. "I'm always here. I'm the teacher."

Everyone stared at me, and my cheeks burned. "I didn't mean you. I meant . . . uh, sorry, Mr. Bunyon."

"Great balls of fire!" Monday exclaimed. "Bunyon's still tormenting students. That square egg once gave me a D on a paper, just because I told him he misclassified the tsetse fly." Monday poked my frog. "Yummy. Frog's legs."

I swatted his hand away.

Mr. Bunyon tapped his pointer on my table. "Is something wrong, Miss Taylor?"

"N-no." I scratched my arm. "It was a mosquito. That frog must have eaten a whole slew of 'em before it pithed."

Mr. Bunyon's eyes nearly crisscrossed.

Monday nudged me. "Want some help slicing that toad?"

I giggled.

Mr. Bunyon tapped his pointer again. "Since you're having such a good time, Miss Taylor, suppose you demonstrate how to dissect a frog."

"Me? But I get hives just slicing roast beef."

"I'll give the instructions, and the class will learn from your mistakes, of which I'm certain there will be a great many." He cleared his throat. "To begin, make an incision with the scalpel at the top of the belly."

Monday stood behind me. "Never fear, your spirit is here." He held my hand around the knife and slit the frog's stomach. My breakfast rose to my throat. I forced myself to look. The frog lay on its back, its legs bent at the joints. Its buggy eyes seemed to stare at me accusingly.

"Next," Mr. Bunyon said, "separate the skin at the incision."

As Monday moved my hands, my fingers touched something rubbery. This time I couldn't look. Instead I stared at some initials carved into the table.

"It's just frog guts, Miranda," Monday said. "Don't croak. Hardy har har. Croak. Get it?"

I groaned. My vision blurred from staring so long at the initials.

Monday's grip on my hand went limp, and I dropped the knife. "Oh, no. The scalpel fell into the frog guts."

The class laughed. I nudged Monday with my elbow, but he seemed to be in a daze. Mr. Bunyon bent over me as far as his stomach would allow.

"Well?" he asked. "Are you going to fetch the scalpel, or just gape at it?"

"You mean, PICK IT UP?"

Monday snapped out of his daze. "Uh-oh, how did that happen?" He picked up the frog and shook it. The scalpel clinked into the tray.

"Yipes," Joey shouted. "Miranda's frog is flying." He jumped up, and his chair slammed into Monday's shin.

"Yeow! That smarts." Monday rubbed his leg, and the frog shot out of his hands.

Larry dashed to pick it up. "Who wants a toad?" He held the frog over his head.

"Me, me," voices chorused.

"Give me that frog," Mr. Bunyon hollered and started chasing him around the room.

Larry tossed the frog to Caroline. She threw it to Joey.

"Jeepers," Monday howled. "It's keep away from Mr. Bunyon time."

Mr. Bunyon made a running leap at Joey, but Joey jumped to the side, and Mr. Bunyon fell over my table.

"Yipes! Watch out!" I zoomed my chair backward as formaldehyde splashed out of my tray.

"Give me that frog," Mr. Bunyon yelled at Joey, who was at the back of the room with his arm held high, ready to throw the frog to someone else.

Monday grabbed it out of Joey's hand. "Okay, Bunyon, you big baby." He carried the frog toward my table.

"Awe-some," Joey said. "Miranda's frog is levitating."

The class screamed and pointed as the frog appeared to float across the room.

"Here ya go, Bunyon," Monday said, dropping the frog into my tray. "Jeepers, you're touchy."

Mr. Bunyon's face was redder than a lobster and all puffed out like a blowfish. "For thirty years I've taught you lunatic adolescents," he raged. "And that's thirty years too many." He stormed out the door just as the last bell rang.

I was still laughing as Linda Sue, Monday, and I headed for my house. I found a note from Mom in the kitchen saying she'd gone to the stationer's. Too bad she hadn't gone to the market. Not even a stale cookie hid in the pantry.

Monday emptied out the last of the Hershey's Kisses I'd bought him on the way home from Julie's yesterday. "Th-th-that's all, folks," he said. "Wanna share?"

Linda Sue stared at the candy. "That is so weird. It's a good thing I know Monday's here, or I'd freak out. The candy looks like it emptied itself out of the bag."

"Oh, yeah," I said. "I keep forgetting you can't see Monday. Listen, he wants to share the Hershey's Kisses with you. I'll use my willpower and pass."

"Thanks, Monday." Linda Sue unwrapped a Hershey's Kiss.

"Listen, Miranda," Monday said. "I'm sorry about dropping that scalpel, but I about had a cat when I saw those initials."

"What initials?" I asked him.

"On the biology table. MN + CH."

"MN plus . . . Ohmigosh. Michael Newberry plus Charlene Hunnicut. You—?"

"—carved those initials," he finished.

"What a bummer," Linda Sue said when I explained.

A pained look marred Monday's handsome face. "Oh well. Forget it," he said. "How about we watch some TV?"

"You're on." I grabbed the mail on the way into the den. "Hey, I got a letter from that Occultomania Shop I wrote to about bat's blood." I read the letter. "Rats. They're sold out."

"Too bad," Linda Sue said. "Maybe your ad in the classifieds will turn up some bat's blood." She giggled. "But I wouldn't hold my breath. People will probably just think your ad is a practical joke."

She had a good point. "Well, I'm going to recheck Madame Lulu. Maybe I missed something about where to find bat's blood." I raced upstairs, grabbed the book, and dashed back into the den.

"Great balls of fire!" Monday shouted. "When did screens get so big? This baby's double the thirteen-inch we had."

When I told Linda Sue what he said, she grinned. "If you think this screen's a biggie," she said to a spot above my right shoulder, "wait until you see my dad's. We're talking humongous."

"Her dad is a video freak," I told Monday. "He's got gadgets you wouldn't believe."

"Cra-zy." Monday stared at the picture coming into focus, and his mouth fell open. "You have color television? They were just coming out with color right before I . . . well, anyway, I always wanted a color TV."

Linda Sue clicked the remote control. The picture flipped to a cartoon show.

"Heyyyy," Monday said. "How did it do that?"

"Click it again, Linda Sue. Monday's never seen remote control."

Monday blinked with each click. "Don't touch that dial," he said as Linda Sue started to punch the clicker again. " 'Leave It to Beaver' is my favorite show. That little Beaver's a scream."

"I hate to break the news, Monday, but that 'little Beaver' grew up. These are reruns."

"What's a rerun?"

I explained, then scanned the appendix in my book, called

"Why Your Potion Fizzled." Halfway down the page, my eyes zeroed in on one word. Liver. "I knew it. Madame Lulu says liver is the pathway to the soul. That must be how I conjured you, Monday."

He grinned. "I wouldn't trust Madame Lulu to boil an egg."

Linda Sue turned down the sound on the TV. "I still say ask Stormy to the Spring Dance, and forget the potion."

"I can't. He might think I like him."

"Isn't that the general idea?"

"Yeah, but what if he already has a date? Maybe he and Julie went back together."

"Excuses, excuses," Monday said. "If a date with Stormy will make you happy, dial him."

"We don't dial anymore," I told him. "We punch." I showed him the phone on Dad's desk.

"Well I'll be." He punched some buttons in the receiver. "Great balls of fire! It plays music."

I grabbed the receiver. "No you don't. With my luck, you'll call Tahiti."

"Phone Stormy and get it over with," Linda Sue said.

I stared at the receiver, trying to think what I could say to Stormy.

"Quit stalling," Linda Sue said.

"Yeah," Monday agreed. "Punch."

"Okay, okay." My fingers trembled as I punched his number.

He answered on the second ring. If I could hear my heart beating, I bet it would sound like a machine gun. "Hi, Stormy," I said. "It's Miranda."

"Hi, Miranda. What's up?"

"Uh, I'm calling you about the Spring Dance. Umm, if you don't have plans . . . I mean, a date, well, I wondered if you might want to go with me?"

"That's really nice of you," he said.

Had he accepted? My heart emptied another round of machine-gun fire.

"The thing is," he said, "I'm Spring Dance King, and it wouldn't be right for me to bring a date. You know. Since so many girls elected me and all."

"Oh. All the girls. Right." My insides seemed to sag.

"But don't worry, Miranda. I'll save you a dance."

"Thanks." I hung up. Nothing seemed to beat, pulse, or course through my body. This must be how dead people felt.

"What did he say?" Linda Sue and Monday asked together.

"He has to spread himself around. Oooh, I'm so embarrassed. I'll never be able to face him again. And I'm not going to that crummy old dance, either."

Monday put his arm around my shoulders. "Heyyyy. You're going if I have to carry you. Besides, I need your help."

"With what?" I sniffed.

"My revenge. I'm getting even with Charlene at the Spring Dance."

Home Movies Always Make Me Cry

8

Monday's revenge eased the pain of Stormy's turning me down for the Spring Dance. When I told Linda Sue what Monday planned, she insisted we buy new formals to wear for the occasion. Only the thought of wearing Adrienne's pukey green hand-me-down made me agree to look.

On Wednesday afternoon, Linda Sue, Monday, and I went to the shopping mall. Monday was bug-eyed at seeing so many shops under one roof. He wanted to go inside every one.

Linda Sue tore into a sack of pretzels. "Let's start on the first level and work our way up."

I shrugged. "Anything you say."

"Lighten up, Miranda. You'll be a real hit at the dance with your chin dragging on the floor."

"Who cares? With my luck, the only boy who'll ask me to dance will be someone like Mom's character Abdul the Desert Rat."

"Abdul's no slouch." Linda Sue licked salt off her fingers. "Besides, we who use our diaries for scratch paper can't afford to be choosy."

I laughed. "We who have only one friend better watch our big mouths."

Monday looked up at the three levels that circled the open center of the mall. "Jeepers. This place is incredible."

"Look—don't touch," I told him. We walked toward the escalators, and I was almost on the first step when Linda Sue detoured me to the center of the mall and a gawking crowd.

She peered over everyone's heads. "I knew being tall would come in handy one day. Isn't this Easter decoration radical?"

"Radical?" Monday repeated. "What's so revolutionary about a stuffed rabbit?"

"Not radical-revolutionary," I said. "Radical-great."

"You mortals sure talk weird." Monday stared at the decoration's centerpiece, a giant rabbit whose head almost reached the second level. The rabbit held a treat-filled basket.

Linda Sue drooled. "Oooh, what I'd give for some of Peter Cottontail's goodies."

"Me, too." I could almost taste the candied Easter eggs and bunny rabbits made of . . .

"Chocolate!" Monday yelled and took a flying leap. "Wings, don't desert me now."

"Come back here," I shouted. "You promised not to touch."

"What's happening?" Linda Sue asked.

"Monday's sitting on the Easter basket. Oh, no. Now he's stuffing chocolate bunnies down his shirt."

Children shrieked with delight as they saw candy fly out of the basket and disappear.

Monday took out a fistful of candy and wound his arm back like a baseball pitcher. "Bombs away!" he yelled and threw a candy hailstorm. The children scrambled after the candy. A security guard blew his whistle.

"Uh-oh, here comes trouble," I told Linda Sue.

When the guard couldn't figure out who was throwing the candy, everyone started laughing.

"Look at those kids," Linda Sue said. "I'll never say an unkind word about a ghost again."

As Monday flew back to us with his shirt full of candy, he rose and sank like a leaky helium balloon.

I giggled. "Well, if it isn't the giant Easter Pig himself."

He chomped off a chocolate rabbit's paw.

"That is so weird," Linda Sue said. "It looks like the bunny's self-destructing."

My gastric juices churned with envy. "Last one to Miller's Department Store is a rotten Easter egg."

I took the escalator two steps at a time, then ran around the second level, past a record store, a video emporium, and a pet shop. I skidded to a halt next to a sign boasting Kincaid's Boutique. Stormy's father owned Kincaid's. I was dying to go inside but scared to at the same time.

Linda Sue jogged toward me, with Monday flying overhead. "Hmmm," she said. "I thought we were going to Miller's, not Kincaid's."

My forehead felt feverish. "Maybe Stormy's working for his dad this afternoon. Please come inside with me. I just *can't* go in by myself."

Linda Sue rolled her eyes. "If I'd known we might run into Stormy, I'd have stayed home and done my homework."

"Ditto," Monday said.

I shoved her in ahead of me and stopped. Stormy was rolling a dress rack loaded with formals across the carpet.

"Hi, Stormy," Linda Sue said, breaking the silence.

"Hi, Stormy," I echoed.

"Miranda!" He jumped behind the dress rack. "What are you doing here?"

My heart beat so fast I think it blanked out my brain. I couldn't think of one reason why we were here.

"We're looking for formals," Linda Sue answered for me.

"Heyyyy." Monday jabbed my side and pointed at a crystal chandelier. "Dig that crazy headlight."

I stared at the chandelier. The crystals cast a golden glint into the floor-to-ceiling mirrors on the walls.

"Awesome, huh?" Stormy said. "Mom bought it in Sweden when we sailed to Europe last summer."

"You sailed on a boat to Europe?"

"A *ship*. The *QE II* isn't exactly an outboard."

"Wow. The closest I ever got to an ocean voyage was taking the ferry to the Statue of Liberty."

Monday laughed. "Don't sweat the small stuff, Miranda. Lover-boy probably lived on seasick pills the whole trip."

Stormy took the gowns from the rack and hung them in one of the cubbyholes built into the walls.

Linda Sue browsed through a few formals. "There's nothing here for me. Ready to go, Miranda?"

"In a minute." I thumbed through the formals Stormy had hung in the cubbyhole.

"Don't do that," he said. "I mean, be careful. My dad will kill me if anything happens to these dresses."

Linda Sue strutted out. "Meet you at Miller's, Miranda."

A man who looked like Stormy opened a door at the back of the boutique. He glanced at me, then at Stormy. "If you're not busy, I could use your help unpacking the new dress shipment."

"Right away, Dad," Stormy said. "I'm not busy." He followed his father into the back. "Call if you need help, Miranda."

Monday made a fist. "Say the word and I'll cream him."

"Don't get uptight, Monday. Stormy probably knows I can't afford these dresses anyway. That's why he didn't stick around."

Monday flicked a tag. "Three hundred dollars for junk like this? I've seen better rags on a hound dog."

"How can you say that? Kincaid's is the most exclusive shop in the mall."

"Says who? Why do you always defend Stormy? Jeepers, Miranda. When will you realize you're a million times cooler than he is? I swear you can't see the trees for the forest."

"That's forest for the trees, and maybe you're the one who needs glasses."

"What's that supposed to mean?"

I looked him flat in his pale blue eyes. "It means, are you sure you want to get revenge on Charlene?"

"What?"

"I said, are you sure—?"

"I heard you. Sure I'm sure. Every time I think how Charlene went after Philpotz, my blood boils. And after *I* sprang for cherry colas at the drive-in, not cheapskate Philpotz. And *I* sat through *Seven Brides for Seven Brothers* twice in a row, just because Charlene had a crush on Howard Keel."

"You mean that old man on 'Dallas'?"

"Howard Keel's in Dallas, Texas?"

"No, it's a TV show."

Monday flicked his comb through his hair. "Anyway, how would you feel if Stormy dumped on you the way Charlene did on me?"

"Stormy and I aren't going together, so he can't dump on me. But you're sure spending a lot of energy getting revenge on someone you hate." I held a blue silk formal up to my chest. "Personally, I wouldn't go to all that trouble, especially when Charlene can't even see you."

"Don't you worry your pretty head. I'll find a way for her

to see me. And you should talk about wasted energy. You're ready to invade a bat cave, just to cast a love spell on a guy whose biggest interest in life is himself. Stormy wouldn't know a wonderful, sweet girl if she knocked him out."

Was Monday calling me sweet and wonderful? My kindergarten teacher once said I was sweet when I didn't squeal on Jimmy Thompson for swiping my new crayons. But nobody ever called me wonderful before.

I hung up the formal. "You're wrong about Stormy. He would too know if a wonderful girl knocked him out."

"Knocked who out?" Stormy pushed through the rear door.

"Oops, uh, I meant this formal is a knockout." I snatched a gown off the rack.

"*That* dress?" Stormy raised an eyebrow.

Monday gasped. "Hang that thing up before it bites you."

I looked at the dress. The black satin gown, with its lace sleeves and high collar, seemed designed for the bride of Frankenstein.

Monday yanked the formal out of my hands.

Stormy blinked. "H-how did you d-do that?"

"Do what?"

"Make the dress hang itself up."

"Really, Stormy. Dresses don't hang themselves up. Have you had your eyes examined lately?"

"I have 20/20 vision." He blinked again.

Monday tapped my shoulder. "Let's split before Linda Sue thinks we forgot about her." He pulled me toward the door.

"Bye, Miranda," Stormy said. "Good luck finding a formal."

Outside Kincaid's, I jerked my arm out of Monday's hand. "Why did you grab that dress from me? Now Stormy probably thinks I'm a basket case *and* a klutz."

"Aw, Miranda. I was just having a little fun."

"Well, stop having fun. My ability to explain unidentified flying objects is running out of fuel, Mon. . . . Monday? Michael Oliver Newberry, materialize this instant." I stared at the air. "Okay, don't show yourself. See if I care."

Some girls snickered at me. "Get *her*," one said.

"Yeah, loony tunes time," another said.

I looked for a manhole to jump into, but there wasn't one in sight. I'd have to stop talking to Monday in public, or people would think I was a space cadet.

My mood plummeted. Now that I thought about it, why should I buy a formal to wear at a dance where I'd probably spend the entire evening blazing a trail from the punch bowl to the ladies' room? I might as well wear Adrienne's pukey green formal.

I was really getting into self-pity when I spotted Linda Sue standing under a closed-circuit television monitor hanging outside a jewelry store. She rubbed on lip gloss and stared moony-eyed at the screen.

I hurried over to her. "What are you looking at? Is someone robbing the jewelry store?"

"Shhh." She pointed at the screen. "Man, these new color monitors are rad. See that blond guy walking up behind us? Is he a hunk or what?"

I looked into the monitor. "Ohmigosh. Linda Sue, remember how you wished you could see Monday?"

"Yeah, but what's that got to do with—"

"That's him."

She dropped her lip gloss. "That's *Monday?* That's really *him?*"

"Did somebody call?" Monday stopped behind me. "Heyyyy, TV. What's on?" He took a step backward. "Holy moly, I am!" He whipped his comb through his hair. "Ah-hem. I'd like to thank my mother, my father, my sixth grade teacher, my—"

"Hold it," I cut in. "Save your speech for the Oscars, Monday. These monitors don't record sound."

Linda Sue gazed at the monitor. "Isn't this a trip, Miranda? I can really see Monday."

"Amazing," Monday said. "Nobody up there told me I could be seen in a . . . Great balls of fire! I'm saved! That's how Charlene can see me. I'll give a speech at the Spring Dance, and tell everyone what a phony Charlene really is. I just need one of these whatchamacallits."

"And a way for people to hear you," I added, then clued Linda Sue in on Monday's idea.

"I've got it," she said. "We can tape Monday with my father's video camera." She pulled me toward the escalator. "Let's go try it out. My folks went to a play, so nobody's home."

"Super idea," I said. "Come on, Monday. We'll give your revenge a test run."

We practically flew to Linda Sue's. She herded us past a wide, circular staircase into her den, where she switched on a set of spotlights.

"This baby records sound," she said, slipping a cassette into a video camera. "So maybe it will pick up your voice, Monday."

I moved Monday in front of the fireplace. "Stand here, so Linda Sue can have a spot to focus the camera on since she can't see you."

"Smart thinking." Monday rested his elbow on the mantel.

"Roll 'em," I said. " 'Monday's Revenge,' take one."

"Ladies and gentlemen," he began, "thirty years ago, I went steady with Charlene Hunnicut, the most popular girl at Garland. But what most of you don't know is, underneath all her beauty, Charlene Hunnicut was a conceited snob, out for numero uno."

I listened to Monday let Charlene have it.

". . . so blindly in love with her that I wouldn't listen when my buddies told me what kind of person she really was."

Monday's words triggered an uncomfortable thought. Linda Sue constantly bugged me about what Stormy was like underneath his good looks. But hey, Stormy isn't a snob like Charlene. He speaks to everyone. Linda Sue's the one who doesn't know the real Stormy.

Monday gave a salute. "So good riddance, Charlene. You and freaky Floyd deserve each other."

"Great speech, Monday," I told him. "He's done, Linda Sue."

She put the cassette from the video camera into the VCR. "Now I'll play the tape back. Keep your fingers crossed that it works."

She flipped a switch on the VCR, and Monday's face appeared on the screen. His pale blue eyes stared out at me. I thought about his going back up there after the Spring Dance. For no reason, my throat ached, and I pushed back tears.

On the screen, Monday opened his mouth and started to speak. "Ladies and gentlemen, thirty years ago . . ." His voice sounded loud and clear.

"It worked," Linda Sue said.

Monday flew into a double flip. "Hallelujah! My problems are solved."

"Radical," I said. "And the video equipment will already be set up at the dance for the old principal's speech. So it's all systems go, Monday."

"Right." Linda Sue rewound the tape. "Whenever you're ready for your revenge, just give Miranda the word, and I'll slip this cassette into the football coach's VCR."

"Will do." Monday plopped on the couch. "Just don't forget to bring that thingamajig to the dance, or Charlene's goose will never get cooked before I have to go back up there."

My stomach knotted. I wished Monday wouldn't keep talking about going back up there, and reminding me he wouldn't be on earth forever.

"It's getting late," I told Linda Sue. "And I have tons of homework."

Monday and I walked to my house. Then he went into the den to read, as he'd been doing every night while I slept.

That night I dreamed Monday was saying good-bye to me and rising toward the sky. I kept trying to pull him back, but every time my hands reached him, a dark, frightening distance came between us.

"Good-byyye, Mirrrranda. . . ." His voice echoed like screams in a canyon. Then he disappeared, and his good-bye faded into a whisper of the wind.

Real Ghosts Don't Play Pac-Man

9

By Friday the good news was I'd made a B + on Tuesday's algebra quiz, thanks to my trusty amulet. The bad news was the afternoon mail brought no reply to my ad for bat's blood. My chances for a meaningful relationship with Stormy were growing dimmer by the minute. I phoned the magic herb and amulet shops listed in the yellow pages, but nobody carried bat's blood.

After scarfing down a quickie dinner, I put on my navy jumpsuit with the red trim. Linda Sue and I were taking Monday to the Donkey Kong Disco, a combination video arcade and teen dance club. I wanted to put a little "fox" into my image in case Stormy was there.

I was just saying good-night to Mom and Dad when Monday materialized at my side. I eased out of the house as he gave me the once-over.

"Heyyyy, where has this ravishing creature been keeping herself all my life?" He wiggled his eyebrows and walked around in a crouch like Groucho Marx.

The thermostat in my cheeks rose several degrees. Kidding or not, Monday was the only boy who'd ever paid me a compliment. He held my hand, and for the first time since he materialized at Dreamland Cemetery, he didn't fly ahead of me. As we walked to Linda Sue's house to pick her up, I paced my footsteps to match Monday's long strides, afraid that if I didn't keep up, he *would* fly ahead.

The sudden heat wave earlier in the week had disappeared, and a scissor-sharp wind cut through the trees and sneaked inside my jumpsuit. I shivered. "Guess I should have worn a sweater, but it will be broiling in the disco."

"Allow me to provide." Monday put his letter sweater around my shoulders. The wool warmed me, but not half as much as his hand in mine had.

Linda Sue came outside practically the minute we rang her doorbell. "Hi, Monday, wherever you are," she said, looking at a spot over my right shoulder. "Boy, you're gonna freak out when you see what video games are." She eyed Monday's letter sweater draped across my shoulders.

"That's weird," I said. "You can see it. Monday, how come Linda Sue can see your sweater on me?"

"Elementary, my dear Miranda. A spirit's clothes can be seen on a mortal. Just not the other way around."

"Gnarly sweater," Linda Sue said when I explained.

Monday looked puzzled. "Is that good?"

"As good as cool, Daddy-o," I told him.

While we walked, it hit me how safe tonight's walk felt compared to the night I went to Dreamland. With Monday near me, the houses appeared merely houses, not ghouls about to pounce on me, and the streetlights formed dancing shadows on the pavement, not eerie moon-monsters.

When I pointed out the Donkey Kong, Monday's eyes widened. The disco was painted pink and purple, and sported a neon sign blinking Donkey Kong in pink and purple lights. Linda Sue opened the door and a rush of warm air greeted us.

I gave Monday back his letter sweater before anyone wondered where I got it. Monday was mesmerized by the rainbow of strobe lights skimming the dance platform in time to the music. A disc jockey sat in a booth playing rock tapes. The disco spilled over with teenagers, either dancing, sitting at tables, or crowding around the soda bar.

I searched the room for Stormy, but didn't see him. Some of my excitement about coming to the disco evaporated.

Monday eyed the gyrating couples. "What in blazes are they doing?"

I giggled and told Linda Sue what Monday said.

She stared at a spot above my right shoulder. "They're doing the Hip Slammer. What dances did you do in the '50s, Monday?"

"Rock 'n' roll, what else?"

I told Linda Sue.

"Sometimes we did the Bop, or the Jitterbug," he added. "All just different kinds of rock 'n' roll." Monday sighed. "But the best was slow dancing."

"You slow-danced?" I asked. "I thought that was a modern dance."

Monday groaned. "We didn't exactly live in the Dark Ages, Miranda. I don't know how you *modern* kids slow-dance, but we used to hold our girl real close while Connie Francis, or Paul Anka, or the Platters sang a romantic song." He smiled. "Some couples didn't even bother to move their feet."

I pictured myself slow dancing with Stormy. He'd hold me tight, his lips would brush my cheek, and then he'd whisper . . .

"Miranda." Linda Sue shook my arm. "Are you comatose? I asked if you wanted to play video games now."

My slow dance fantasy fizzled. "Yeah. Let's go for it."

We threaded our way through the crowd into another room where rows of video machines stood at attention like a military drill team. *Bams*, *beeps*, and *pings* accompanied flashing colored lights shooting out of the machines.

Monday's eyes sparkled as bright as the lights. "Okay, what do we do with these crazy slot machines?"

"Which game should we teach Monday?" I asked Linda Sue.

She scanned the room, then zipped down an aisle and skidded to a halt in front of an unoccupied machine.

"Perfect," I shouted. "Pac-Man!"

Linda Sue looked above my shoulder again. "No offense, Monday, but the goal in Pac-Man is to zap those little things running around the board. They're called, uh, ghosts."

Monday scrutinized the screen. "Those little doohickeys don't look like any spirits I know."

I explained the rules and how to use the joystick, then dropped a couple of quarters into the machine. The *wuka-wuka* sound blasted on, and the ghosts sprang into action.

"Watch out," Linda Sue hollered. "That blue ghost is about to zap Pac-Man."

Monday rammed down the joystick. I stood behind him and placed my hands on his. All I needed was for someone to think I was making Pac-Man play by itself.

"Way to go," Linda Sue said as Monday zapped a pink ghost.

He frowned. "But they keep coming back."

"That's life in the fast lane," I teased. "Hang in there."

He did. In about ten seconds, the animated happy face had eaten all the dots.

Linda Sue jumped up and down. "You won on your first try."

"You're terrific," I chimed in.

Monday flew into a double flip. "Great balls of fire! Let's play again."

I threw my head back and laughed . . . right into a pair of dreamy brown eyes. "Hi, Stormy," I said, as a million caterpillars turned into flittering butterflies inside me. Stormy stared from my curls down to my feet. Now I knew what Mom meant when she wrote, "His eyes undressed her." I crossed my arms over my chest.

"You look pretty," Stormy said. "I never saw you so, uh, dressed up."

"Thanks. You look pretty nice, too." His tan cords and shirt made his eyes look like brown velvet.

From the disco room the deejay's voice boomed over the microphone. "Listen up, everyone. The moment you girls have been waiting for has *arrived*."

"Later," Stormy said. "Gotta check out the action."

"It's a ladies' choice." Linda Sue almost yanked my shoulder out of its socket as she dragged me into the disco room.

"Ow. Slow down," I told her. "I like having two arms."

"Sorry, Miranda, but ladies' choices are the only times I get to dance with someone whose nose doesn't jab me in the chin."

Monday floated through the crowd of people, while Linda Sue and I squinched our way toward the disc jockey standing on the dance platform.

"Line up against the soda bar," he said, "scope out your favorite guy, and, when I give the signal, go get him."

I spotted Stormy standing with some jocks on Garland's baseball team. "Oh no!" I moaned.

"What's the matter?" Linda Sue asked.

"Look who just slithered up to Stormy."

"Gross. What snake hole did Julie Phillips crawl out of?"

Julie whispered something in Stormy's ear, then slinked up to the soda bar, a smug grin on her face. A red-haired girl wearing skintight jeans and a low-cut blouse blew a kiss to Stormy on her way to line up, and then two more raving beauties signaled to him. I felt like a prune in the middle of a bunch of grapes.

Linda Sue angled me toward the soda bar. "Don't worry, Miranda. You can outrun the competition any day."

"I think I'll pass."

"Why?" Monday asked. "I thought you wanted to dance with Stormy."

"I do, but I'd just die if he said no, like he did about the Spring Dance."

"He won't," Linda Sue assured me. "A guy has to accept the first girl who asks him. Ladies' choice rules."

"Never fear," Monday said. "Your spirit is here. I don't dig your choice, but maybe if you dance with Stormy, you'll get that male Mata Hari out of your system."

"On your mark," the disc jockey said, "get set, *go!*"

"CHARGE!" Monday hollered and pushed me ahead of the girls running toward Stormy. "Quick, ask him to dance."

"Uh, Stormy, do you"—a flash of red, followed by one of chestnut, caught my eye—"want to dance?" I finished as Julie and the red-haired girl reached us.

Julie's eyes shot daggers at me. "I should have known Muscles here would win a *race*."

The redhead grinned. "Watch out, Julie. Your fangs are showing."

Julie's mouth dropped open as if a barbell had fallen on her toes.

"Don't worry, girls," Stormy said. "I'll dance with you two later."

The music started playing a slow dance, and Stormy wrapped his arms around me. I tried not to breathe, scared he'd feel me gasping from being so close to him. Maybe if I said something clever, I'd calm down.

"The Donkey Kong is a rad place," I tried. Great, Miranda. That insightful observation should get the old conversational ball rolling.

"Yeah," Stormy answered. "But I don't remember seeing you here before."

"You probably just didn't notice me." Even better, Miranda. Tell him you're an unnoticeable type. My Stormy fantasy had finally come true, and my mouth was stuck in terminal lockjaw.

Stormy pressed his lips next to my ear. "Your hair smells good."

My nervous system sent enraptured signals throughout my body. Stormy smelled like Christmas. I stared at his neck. If I looked into his eyes a second longer, I'd melt into a puddle at his feet and probably ruin his shoes.

"It's hard to believe you're such a good dancer," he said. "I mean, you seem different tonight. Not like at the pizza parlor." He tightened his arm around my waist.

I tightened mine around his shoulders. We were barely dancing now, just swaying to the music. What did Mom's heroines do in situations like this? All that flashed through my mind was what Ashley Bowen did in *Savage Lover*. I massaged Stormy's shoulders.

He made sounds like Linda Sue's cat did when she spied a dish of cream. "Gosh, I never thought I'd want to—"

A girl screamed.

Want to what? My heart begged him to go on. But the girl

screamed again and Stormy turned us toward the voice. It was Julie. A big guy with long stringy hair was hassling her.

Julie struggled in the boy's grip. "Get your hands off me!" she hollered.

Stormy's hand stiffened in mine. I thought he was going to clobber the guy, but he just stared at him and Julie as if he were watching a movie.

The guy bent Julie backward and kissed her. She twisted her head and tried to bite him. He whipped her arms behind her back.

For some crazy reason, I wanted to help her.

"Miranda, stop!" Linda Sue shouted as I ran toward Julie. "Do you want to get killed?"

"I'll help," the red-haired girl shouted, catching up to me.

"If you can't beat 'em, join 'em," Linda Sue shouted and joined a bunch of girls running toward Julie and the boy.

A half-empty glass of chocolate soda sat on a table. I snatched it and threw the gooey stuff at the boy's face.

"What the? . . ." He let go of Julie and wiped his shirttail across his eyes.

While he was temporarily blinded, the other girls and I shoved him across the room and out the door. He stumbled across the parking lot to a motorbike. Then he revved the engine and sped into the street.

Everyone shouted, "Yay," and some people whistled.

Monday clapped me on the back. "Great balls of fire! I couldn't have handled that hood better myself."

I just grinned at him.

"Thanks, you guys," Julie said. "What a creep."

"Were we terrific, or what?" Linda Sue asked.

"More than terrific," the redhead said. "Did you see how that guy took off?"

Linda Sue and I started giggling, and we didn't stop until

we'd walked from the Donkey Kong back to her house. She went inside, and then Monday held my hand as we walked on to my house.

In spite of the cold night air, I felt warm all over. I rehashed the events at the Donkey Kong. Suddenly a pang hit my conscience, and my warm feeling disappeared. How could I be gasping for breath one minute while slow-dancing with Stormy, and tingly warm the next minute while Monday held my hand? Then another thought hit me. Why hadn't Stormy clobbered that bully?

I was digging my house key out of my purse when Adrienne exploded onto the porch and waved an envelope in my face.

"This just came for you," she gasped. "Special delivery telegram. I signed for it."

"Special delivery!" My hands shook so hard when I read the message I ripped a corner of the paper. The telegram was from Mr. Ogelthorpe. BE AT SWAP MEET TOMORROW, it said. BAT'S BLOOD ARRIVED TONIGHT.

The Bat Connection

10

Early Saturday morning, Monday and I went to Hamilton College Stadium.

"Holy Toledo!" Monday exclaimed when he saw the booths crammed from goalpost to goalpost.

"This zoo is your basic swap meet," I told him as we made our way onto the football field. "Let's find Mr. Ogelthorpe first, and then we can browse around the other booths."

"You really want to waste time looking for this guy?" Monday asked.

"It's not a waste of time. I have to get real bat's blood for my love potion."

"Hogwash. But I can tell I'll never convince you, so what does this Ogelthorpe look like?"

"Sort of tall, I think. It was hard to get a good look at him while he chased me across the school parking lot. Just help me find a magic amulet booth. That's what he sold at school."

"Okay. Let's move 'em on out." Monday took flight.

I hoofed it, dodging mothers armed with baby strollers,

kids loaded with melting ice cream cones, and bargain hunters steamrolling their way to the booths as if the owners of the booths were giving away original Picassos.

"Heyyy. Dig these aquariums," Monday hollered and swooped toward a tropical fish booth. "I always wanted a piranha."

"Don't touch those fish," I warned him.

"I didn't." A young boy raised his arms as if I'd said, "Stick 'em up."

"Good going, kid," I bluffed.

He gave me a strange look, then ran off.

"No handling the merchandise," I muttered to Monday. "A security guard might accuse me of shoplifting."

"A piranha?" Monday roared.

I laughed, too, the idea sounded so crazy.

We went past booths selling kitchen gadgets, handwoven rugs, beat-up furniture, and other used junk. When we were almost to the far goalpost, I saw a table loaded with small boxes containing gemstones of every color and size. I moved closer, and a tall man with an emaciated mustache slithered up to me.

"May I help you?" he asked.

"Are you Mr. Ogelthorpe?" I asked.

"The same. And I remember you, Miss Taylor." He eyed my shoulder bag. "Got my amulet in there?"

I stepped back. "First let's see your bat's blood."

"Smart thinking," Monday said.

Mr. Ogelthorpe reached under the table and brought out a small bottle. "Okay, let's have the amulet."

"Not so fast." I unscrewed the cap, and a vaguely familiar odor seeped out. "Are you sure this is real bat's blood?"

"The purest," Mr. Ogelthorpe swore, sweat trickling down his bony neck.

Monday sniffed. "Let me see that bottle." He held it up to the sun.

Mr. Ogelthorpe's beady eyes bugged out. "H-how did you do that?"

"Uh, I ah . . ."

Monday slammed the bottle on the table, and orange liquid spurted out.

"Watch it!" I hollered. "You're spilling my bat's blood."

"I never touched that bottle," Mr. Ogelthorpe said.

Monday glowered at him. "I believe you, pal. You wouldn't want to stain your hands with Mercurochrome."

"Mercurochrome. I knew this stuff smelled familiar." I started to walk away.

"Wait," Mr. Ogelthorpe called. "I can explain."

"I told you, no bat's blood, no deal."

"Yeah, plant ya now, dig ya later," Monday said as we marched away. "Great balls of fire! You were a cool cat, Miranda. I'm glad you didn't let him con you, although your amulet might have been conned off someone else."

"You think Mr. Ogelthorpe stole the onyx?"

"Could be. He's sure in a tizzy to get it back. I don't think he believes it's charmed, though. That amulet's not worth a plugged nickel in the magic department."

"But I conjured you with this amulet."

"Circumstantial evidence. It was the Night of the Wishes, remember?"

I knelt down and pretended to tie my shoelaces. "But I held this onyx in my hand that night," I mumbled toward my tennis shoes.

Monday laughed. "You could have held cow manure, and it wouldn't have made any difference. I told you what the rules said. You were the one who stood at my grave at midnight, so whatever magic there was came from you."

I shook my head.

He spread his arms and looked at the sky. "Help. It's like this, Miranda. No*body* and no *thing* is gonna put you on easy street. You have to make your wishes come true yourself."

The black onyx glittered in my hand. Easy street. Is that what Stormy falling in love with me would mean? Monday could be right, but just in case he wasn't, I put the amulet in my coin purse and shoved it down to the bottom of my big shoulder bag. "I'll think about it," I told him.

"Suit yourself." Monday flew ahead. In a minute, he nose-dived to a booth on the boundary line of the football field and held up a pair of loafers. "Great balls of fire! White bucks!"

I grabbed the shoes. "Now watch my lips. There is a man over there eyeing me suspiciously. Do you know why? Because, like any normal human being, he has never seen a pair of shoes TAKE FLIGHT!"

Monday jumped. "Okay, okay. But please, Miranda, just find out how much the bucks cost."

The look on his face was like that of a little boy begging for a lollipop, and I couldn't resist. "All right. Wait here." I left him singing a song about a white sport coat and a pink carnation.

The man who'd stared at me chomped on a wad of tobacco and clutched a cigar box. "Shoes cost two seventy-five," he said when I asked the price.

"Make it a dollar, and you've got a deal."

"Two dollars," he countered. "Them bucks are gen-u-wine leather. Not your imitation Pat Boones."

"Pat Boones? Is that a good brand?"

"Don't get smart with me, girlie." He spit out the wad of tobacco. "A dollar seventy-five. That's my last offer."

"Sold!" I slapped the money into his hand.

"Want a bag?" he asked, stuffing the money into his cigar box.

"No, thanks." I had a better idea. I'd put the shoes in my shoulder bag and surprise Monday with them later. I slouched my shoulders and lumbered back to him trying to look disappointed.

"How much did the guy want?" Monday asked.

I stared at the ground so he wouldn't see me smile. "A fortune. I'm sorry, Monday."

"Thanks for trying." He looked so forlorn I was tempted to give him the white bucks right then.

We walked by some more booths, not saying anything. Then Monday dashed ahead of me and ducked into a tent selling records.

"Heyyyy, dig these platters." He pulled a forty-five out of its wrapper.

"Don't touch that." I grabbed the record.

"Hey, that's Buddy Holly." Monday strummed an imaginary guitar. "I love you, Peggy Sue," he sang. "Buddy Holly was the coolest. We used to dance to 'Peggy Sue' at all the sock hops."

I had a mental picture of a bunch of socks hopping around.

"Hey, girl," a man yelled and ran up to me. "Can't you read? The sign says, Don't Handle the Merchandise."

I put the record back, and the man shuffled off to wait on a customer.

"The old grump," Monday said and took out the record again.

"What's wrong with you? Didn't you hear what he said?"

"Who ya talkin' to, girl?" the man asked. "You got an accomplice helping you lift my merchandise while I'm not looking?"

"No, sir. I uh, was just excited to find a Boddy Hully, a Buddy Holly."

He narrowed his eyes. Some little kids ran up and started attacking the record shelves. The man turned his wrath on them.

"Aaagh!" Monday clutched his chest.

"What's wrong?" Did ghosts have heart attacks?

Monday held up another record. "I found Charlene's and my song."

I put the record back and pulled him behind the tent where no one could see me talking to him. "You screamed bloody murder over a *record*?" I asked.

"Not just any record. That was 'Love Me Tender,' Charlene's and my song." He knelt at my feet. "Please, Miranda? Buy this one record for me? Elvis Presley is my idol."

"Was," I corrected him.

"Huh?"

"A person who died can't *be* your idol. That person *was* your idol."

Monday looked as if he were having a tooth pulled without Novocain. "No! Not Elvis! Tell me it isn't true."

"I thought you'd know. You said spirits can see what's happening on earth."

"We can, but I must have missed Elvis's exit when I stopped spying on earth."

"Maybe you'll run into him when you"—I forced myself to complete the sentence—"go back."

"Are you kidding? Do you know how many spirits live up there? The only stars I've ever seen are in the Big Dipper." Monday rested his chin in his hands. "Lay it on me, Miranda. Who else passed through while I wasn't looking? Is Chuck Berry still around? Fats Domino? Little Richard?"

"I never heard of them. Listen. Why don't I find out how much that guy wants for the Elvis record?"

"Oh, Miranda. Would you?"

"Be right back."

The dollar fifty the man asked was worth the price to see Monday smile again.

"How about the comic book?" the man asked.

"What comic book?"

"The one you're hiding behind your back. What have you got on that sweatshirt, Velcro?"

I reached behind me and felt a pair of hands. "Monday!"

"Wrong," the man said. "*Archie.*"

"Just one more souvenir," Monday said. "I haven't read an *Archie* in decades."

The man dug inside his shirt and pulled out a whistle attached to a chain. "Okay, sister, I knew you were up to no good."

"Uh-oh," Monday said. "He's blowing the whistle on us. Let's make like a tree and leave." He pulled me across the football field as a small army of security guards chased after us.

The Not-So-Good, Good Old Days

11

My legs had never moved so fast in my life. "Drop that comic book," I told Monday, hoping a guard would pick it up, so I wouldn't spend the rest of my life hiding a shoplifting record.

We ran out of the stadium and cut into the parking lot. I crawled under a motor home, while the guards weaved between parked cars like the Keystone Cops.

After what seemed like hours, Monday reported they'd gone. We ran like marathoners to the bus stop. By the time we got home, the sun was a flaming ball of red, sinking toward the horizon. Adrienne sat on the front porch painting her nails.

"Hi ya, Adrienne," I called. "What's happening?"

"Shhh." She held a frosty pink nail up to her lips and nodded toward the attic window. "You'll disturb Mom. When I came downstairs, she was yelling, 'You wretch! Why did I ever believe you loved me?'"

"Heyyyy," Monday said. "Your daddy-o seemed like a cool

cat to me. Just goes to show you can't trust first impressions."

I giggled. "Mom's making progress on her new *book*," I said for Monday's benefit. "Sounds like she's up to the old heroine-doubts-hero's-love-for-her scene."

"Yeah." Adrienne spread on another coat of polish. "Where'd you get that record?"

I stared at the forty-five in my hand like I'd just seen it. "Uh, at the swap meet."

She peered at the title. " 'Love Me Tender'? Isn't that kinda old fashioned?"

"Heyyyy," Monday said. "What're you calling old fashioned?"

"I'm on a nostalgia trip today," I told Adrienne.

"By the way," she said. "Stormy phoned while you were gone."

I gasped. "What did he say? Is he going to call me back? Does he want me to call him back?"

"Don't get hyper. He just phoned to tell me he and Julie had another fight, and she broke her date with him for Saturday after the Spring Dance. They were supposed to double with Ben and me to see that new movie, *E.T. Phones Outer Mongolia*."

"I don't get it," Monday said. "Why would Elizabeth Taylor phone Outer Mongolia?"

"Shhh. I mean, we better talk softer. Mom's book, you know. So go on. What else did Stormy say?"

"Not much. He just asked me to get him another date. He has a term paper due, and he doesn't have time to phone a lot of girls to see who doesn't have a date for that Saturday."

"A date. Oh, Adrienne, please. Fix me up with Stormy."

Monday clicked his tongue. "Tsk tsk. Groveling at your sister's feet."

If groveling meant a date with Stormy, I'd grovel all the way to China. "Say yes, Adrienne. Please?"

"Psst." Monday came close to my ear. "I hate to give you a way to go out with Stormy, but if it will make you happy . . ."

I nodded.

"Offer her something in exchange," Monday said.

Super idea. I'd make her an offer she couldn't refuse. "Listen, Adrienne. If you get Stormy to take me out, I'll wash your clothes for a week."

She looked doubtful.

"Then I'll do your homework, take your nights to wash dishes, clean up your room."

"Stay out of my room."

"Then what *can* I do?"

Adrienne blew on her nails. A cagey look slinked across her face. "You can be in the Drama Club skit for the Spring Dance."

"But Adrienne, I'm a total klutz at dancing, and you've heard me sing. Off-key is an understatement."

"So mouth the words. Unless, of course, you don't want a date with Stormy."

"I do, I do. You win. Rats. Now I *will* be an April Fools' joke, and recorded on Coach Brody's videotape, too. I'll never be able to destroy my klutzy image."

"Those are the breaks," Adrienne said. "I'll phone Steph to count on you. She's in charge of the skit." Adrienne held her wet nails out like claws, and twisted the doorknob with two fingers. "You'll love the skit. They're singing those corny but cute songs from the '50s."

"Heyyyy," Monday said as she went inside. "Your sister insulted my good old days. Just wait till I tell the folks up there about her."

My nerves snapped. "All you talk about is the good old days. What makes the 'good old days' so good anyway?"

Monday opened his mouth, but nothing came out.

I wished I could chop off my tongue. "I'm sorry. It's just that the 1980s are neat, too. We have home computers and Walkman radios and microwaves, and lots of things you haven't even seen yet."

Monday leaned against the porch railing. "Maybe I'm just stuck in the age I grew up in. For me, the '50s had everything. Black-and-white television was the invention of the century, and a hi-fi was the top of the line in phonographs." He stared across our front yard, his brow furrowing into wrinkles. "I wish I'd lived to enjoy more of those years."

My legs moved toward Monday of their own volition, and my arms automatically circled his waist. I wasn't even embarrassed. Around Monday was just the most natural place in the world for my arms to be. He hugged me back, and tingles danced inside me.

"Boy, am I the original Great Pretender." He stopped hugging me, but kept his hands on my shoulders. "I brag about the '50s like that decade was the golden age of civilization. The truth is the good old days weren't always good. Did I tell you my dad was killed in the Korean War?"

I shook my head. "But don't you see your dad . . . up there?"

"Yeah, but for some reason, here on earth I feel sad, like I did then. I think my mother never got over Dad's death, because she died two years later." Monday steered me to the porch steps, and we sat next to each other. "We played the stupidest game in the '50s," he went on. "Called Chicken. Two guys got in their cars and raced each other toward a drop-off. The first one to put on the brakes lost. Great balls of fire! Anybody with one brain cell working shoulda realized the real winner was the chicken."

Monday's eyes seemed vacant, as if he were racing toward that drop-off right now. I hooked my arm through his, and we sat on the porch steps until the red sun turned into a pumpkin sun, sliding down pink and orange streamers toward its bed in the horizon.

On Sunday I got up early. Adrienne's friend Steph, the skit leader everyone called the Commandant, had scheduled a rehearsal for eight o'clock. Three hours later I limped home with a stabbing pain in my thighs from doing a billion high kicks while singing "oooh waa diddy" until I thought my voice box would croak.

Monday waited for me in my room. "I see you had a terrific skit rehearsal," he teased.

"Hardy har har. For someone who gets instant paralysis at the mention of exercise, I should be awarded the Purple Heart for motion beyond the endurance of my body."

He laughed. "Come on. I'll show you my old haunts and take your mind off the skit."

"Oh, that's right. We were going to visit your old neighborhood today."

After a twenty-minute bus ride, Monday pulled the cord, and the bus swerved to a stop in front of a coin laundry. I'd only been in this section of town a few times before. The small shops facing the cobbled street seemed out of another time. We walked past one-story houses, all identical except for different-color paint. Bicycles, tricycles, and Big Wheels littered tiny front yards. Nobody else was around, and the neighborhood seemed deserted.

All at once Monday stopped in front of a vacant lot overgrown with weeds. "Heyyyy. Where's my house?"

"Are you sure we're on the right street?"

"Of course I'm sure. Someone must have torn it down. How could they do that?" He scooped up a fistful of pebbles and threw them at the vacant lot. Then he charged across the street. I hobbled after him up another block.

"Great balls of fire! See that man pumping gas? That's Tex. I used to work for him after school."

I watched the man with the shock of white hair bend over a gas nozzle as if the hose weighed a ton.

Monday shook his head. "When I worked for Tex, he had jet black hair, and everybody called him Mr. Muscle. I wish he could see me. I really dug that guy."

A sports car screeched into the station, and a girl in jeans hopped out. "Yo, Tex," she called and hefted a gas nozzle toward her tank.

Monday's mouth dropped open. "What's she doing?"

"Filling up."

"A girl?"

"Yes, a *girl*." I turned my back to the street, so nobody at the gas station would see me talking to Monday. "I told you. Today girls do the same jobs boys do."

Monday frowned. "I should have known the country would go to the dogs without me around." He grinned. "So what do you say we mosey on up the road to my drive-in movie?"

"I'm with you, pardner."

We passed a hardware store, a pharmacy, and a pet shop, all of which practically swallowed up the narrow street. Stomach-melting odors sifted out of one shop bearing the sign, Gordon's Home-Baked Pastries.

Monday licked his lips. "Here's one place that didn't change. Mom always said I ate so many of Mrs. Gordon's chocolate eclairs they were growing outta my ears."

I peered at his ears, then put my hand over my mouth and whispered, "Your mom was right. There's a sliver of eclair behind your left lobe."

"Really? Aw, you're kidding." He angled me to the right. "Now, madam, if you'll kindly look straight ahead, you'll see the number one parking place of the '50s, and I don't mean a place to park your car. Hardy har har. This is the Royal Drive . . . -in. Oh no."

I followed his gaze to a sign on top of a tall pole. Smashed lightbulbs in the shape of an arrow zigzagged across the sign, pointing toward a giant movie screen that towered over the parking area. The voice boxes were gone, leaving short poles lined up in neat rows, like a cavalry of headless horsemen. Only the ticket booth remained intact, hovering in front of the deserted drive-in, as if safeguarding a holy shrine.

There was a notice on the ticket booth window. "That's incredible. Did movies really cost a quarter?"

Monday nodded. "How much does a movie cost today?"

"Would you believe as much as six bucks?"

"Holy Toledo." He exhaled a rush of air. "There used to be a fence around the parking lot, but somebody must have torn it down. Like my house. The mayor should declare this drive-in a national monument to the '50s. Then no one could ever tear it down."

I wished I could do something to cheer him up. "Say, how about an old-fashioned chocolate sundae at your drive-in hamburger place?"

"Chocolate? You're on." He glanced over his shoulder at the movie screen. "I guess one out of three ain't bad."

We'd walked about two more blocks when Monday pointed ahead, his hands trembling.

"What have they done to Carlson's Burger Barn?" he demanded. "Where's the wooden shack kitchen, and the pink-striped awning? What happened to the carhops on roller skates?" He pressed his fingers against his temples. "Has all my past dematerialized, just like me?"

I stared in the direction Monday pointed, and my soul turned over. The place still sold hamburgers, but no waitresses roller-skated around parked cars, taking people's orders. Now customers ate inside at tables, not in their cars. The wooden shack with the pink-striped awning had been turned into a red-brick eatery. And curving high over the roof of the eatery perched a pair of golden arches.

12

When I told Monday what a McDonald's was, his mood plummeted. He spent the next three days revisiting his old neighborhood, trying to get over the shock of seeing his past obliterated. I spent most of those days running between school, skit rehearsal, and the library. I looked up sources for bat's blood, but all I learned was bats have warm blood.

By Thursday afternoon, I was desperate. The Spring Dance was tomorrow night. I checked Madame Lulu's book for love spells that didn't call for impossible potion ingredients. I found only one.

Holding my breath, I put the chicken gizzard, raw egg, and dead fish head into a bowl. Then I lit a candle, rubbed my amulet for luck, and chanted the incantation:

> *Oh, spirits of love, give a nod,*
> *Make Stormy Kincaid crave my bod;*
> *For setting my Stormy's passion going,*
> *Here's a batch of your favorite potion.*

I emptied the potion into a garbage can outside, wishing Monday would hurry back. Counting today, he had only three days left before his two weeks on earth would be up. I fell into a kitchen chair feeling depressed and confused. How could I be moaning about Monday's leaving, when I'd just cast a love spell on Stormy?

The front door slammed and Mom came into the kitchen. In a flash, she unloaded the week's supply of groceries. Even wearing cutoffs and an ink-stained sweatshirt, Mom was beautiful. Today she'd pinned her thick blonde hair up high on her head.

A frown knotted her forehead. "Miranda, my sweet, why the sad face?"

I swear Mom has ESP. She always knows when I'm feeling down. "I was just thinking about the Spring Dance," I told her. "I don't exactly have a date." I couldn't tell her I was trying to decide between loving a boy two years older than me or a ghost.

She took my hand. "We haven't had one of our girl talks in a long time. Come with me."

I let her pull me into the den, and I nuzzled close to her on the sofa, feeling about half my fourteen years.

"Now tell me," she said, "what's bothering you?"

"Oh, it's just that boys never ask me to dances or movies or anything. What's wrong with me?"

"There's nothing wrong with you, Miranda. Some girls are just slow starters. I didn't have a lot of dates at first, either."

"You didn't? But you're so pretty."

"And you're pretty, too. It amazes me how you can't see that. But you know what? There'll be lots more dances. I can't promise you'll have dates for all of them, but I bet you'll have your fair share. And if you don't, you'll survive."

"How can I survive, when I'm practically the only girl in my class who never gets asked out? Linda Sue's getting close, I just know it."

Mom laughed. "Miranda, you're the champ of hyperbole. I've chaperoned a few of those dances, and I *think* I noticed one or two other girls without dates." She mussed my hair. "One thing I know for sure. And that is I love you very much." She tickled my ribs the way she used to when I'd come home from kindergarten crying that the most awful thing in the whole entire world had happened to me.

"Uncle, uncle." I giggled.

Mom stopped tickling me. "Wait a minute. I have a surprise for you."

"For me? What is it?"

"You'll see. I hope it proves I'm not always glued to my typewriter." She ran upstairs, and in a second her feet pattered back down.

"Hurry," I called. "I can't stand the sus— *Adrienne's formal?*"

Mom swept the pukey green gown under my nose. "I cut off those ruffles around the hemline you didn't like, and lowered the neckline."

"Oh. Now I see the difference." I didn't want to hurt her feelings by saying the daring slash she cut in the neck would just about reveal my collarbones.

"Why don't you try it on?" she suggested.

"Try it on. Right." I peeled off my jeans and T-shirt, then slipped on the gown. I looked at myself in the hall mirror. Without the ruffles, Adrienne's formal was only half gross. Mom had even taken in the skirt just enough so my "pleasingly plump" hips, as Dad called my fatty tissues, didn't appear gargantuan.

"What's the verdict?" Mom asked.

"It sure is different." What else could I say with her hovering over me? "How come you never told me you could sew?"

"You never asked me." She gave me the once-over. "Not bad, if I do say so myself." She sighed. "Gee, I remember going to my first formal at Garland. I spent about six hours getting ready, I was so excited."

Yipes. Mom went to Garland, too. What if she knew Monday? I had to know. "Mom, uh, when did you graduate high school?"

"Don't ask. Oh what the heck, ask. Nineteen sixty-two. A very good year." She counted by tens on her fingers. "Heavens. I can't believe I'll be celebrating my thirtieth reunion in nineteen . . . Well, let's just say sometime during this century."

"Oh, Mom." I didn't know whether I was glad or not that she wasn't at Garland when Monday was. If they'd been classmates, maybe she could have told me more about him. "But you were *around* in the '50s. Were those years really as good as everyone says?"

"Who's everyone? I didn't know you had friends that old— I mean, who grew up in the '50s."

"I don't. It's just that, uh, the deejays are playing '50s songs now and calling them oldies but goodies."

A smile inched across Mom's lips. "Yes. The '50s *were* the good old days. But they were more than rock'n'roll, or Elvis, or sock hops. There was a quality of innocence during those years, a kind of carefree fun that will never happen again."

"Innocence?" I asked. "I don't understand."

"Hmmm. How do I explain?" Mom sat on the bottom stair

step and pulled the pins out of her hair. It fell in waves around her shoulders. "I guess by carefree innocence, I mean how can '50s love songs about holding hands in the moonlight or pep rallies around bonfires ever sound exciting, when you kids see wars going on, and people getting assassinated, and thousands of homeless people sleeping in the streets, just by reading a paper or turning on the television?"

Mom stared into space, and the same faraway expression glazed her eyes that misted Monday's whenever he drifted into thoughts about the '50s.

I touched her arm. "Mom? Are you okay?"

"What? Oh, yes, I'm fine." She started upstairs. "I'm off to the salt mines again. Got to get Hillary and the baron on their way to living happily ever after."

Happily ever after. What would it be like to live happily ever after with Stormy? Or Monday? But Monday is a ghost. Did I want to spend the rest of my life with a spirit? Monday's and Stormy's images tumbled around in my head like clothes in a washing machine. I wondered how I'd ever make up my mind which boy I really loved. Then I worried whether the one I chose would love me. I think happily ever after only happens in romance novels.

I was still pondering which boy I loved best at the Spring Dance Friday night. Then stage fright pushed my already hyped-up nervous system into overload. We were supposed to do the skit right after Coach Brody finished showing the videotape of Garland's former principal's speech.

To top it off, our costumes looked like they'd come out of a circus. We wore gray felt skirts with pink poodles stitched on them, pink pullover sweaters with V necks, white socks rolled down to our ankles, and these brown-and-white shoes with laces, called saddle Oxfords. My poodle skirt itched, and my pink sweater looked like it had grown two sizes since dress rehearsal. I wondered if I'd accidentally put on the "full-bodied" pullover of the girl standing next to me. Hers seemed tight. I scratched my hips like a chimpanzee, much to the disgust of the Commandant, our esteemed skit director.

Linda Sue stood beside me behind the makeshift stage in the gym. She looked beautiful in a lavender formal.

"Nothing to be nervous about," she said. "You'll knock 'em dead."

"Easy for you to say. I'm the one who's about to make a clown of herself in front of the whole entire student body, not to mention my heart's desire."

"Oh, and where is *Monday*?"

I shot her one of my scathing looks. "I meant *Stormy*. As for Monday, he was so hyper about seeing Charlene he went for a flight to calm down. He's meeting us here."

"I can't wait. This will be the first formal I'll have something to do besides sit around praying that even a nerd will ask me to dance."

Linda Sue's humor didn't zap even one of my jitterbugging butterflies. "Do you have the videocassette to play of Monday's revenge speech?"

"Safe and sound in my purse." She took out a small tape recorder. "And the Elvis record I taped is right here, ready to belt out, 'Love Me Tender.' All we need now is Monday."

I sniffed for chocolate odors, but smelled only different perfume scents. I peeked around the curtain, hoping to see Stormy. I saw Adrienne and Ben sitting at one of the tables near the dance floor, but no Stormy.

Linda Sue peered over my shoulder. "Check out the decorations. Adrienne's committee did a rad job."

"I hate to admit it, but you're right." The decorations in blue and gold, Garland's school colors, hung everywhere, from the pom-poms circling the basketball hoops to the crepe paper frames encasing photographs of 1950s movie idols and recording stars.

A flurry of voices interrupted the former principal's video-taped speech.

"Ohmigosh," Linda Sue exclaimed. "I think it's *her*."

People swarmed around the entrance, shouting hellos to Mr. Phillips and a woman walking in with him.

"She has to be Charlene," I said. "Who else would appear in public with Floyd Phillips?"

The woman wore a black sequined chemise, and her blonde hair was tied into a French knot. A real beaut, as Monday would say, even after thirty years.

Mr. Phillips seated Charlene at the table closest to the stage. The whirling silver ball on the ceiling cast a spotlight on her, revealing wisps of gray hair mixed in with the blonde, and squiggly lines at the edges of her expertly made-up eyes.

"Oh, dear," I said to Linda Sue. "I hope Monday isn't too shocked when he sees Charlene doesn't look like the young girl in his yearbook."

She sighed. "Charlene's not a Spring Chicken Queen anymore, is she?"

"Uh-uh. Yipes. There's Stormy. Wow. I've never seen him in a tux before."

Linda Sue faked a yawn. "Big deal. Look, here comes Her Royal Highness, Queen Julie."

"Rats. And she looks terrific, too."

Julie slinked in wearing a strapless powder blue formal with a straight skirt. She and Stormy sat with Charlene and

Mr. Phillips. I confess my eyes saw green. But my nose smelled chocolate.

"Heyyyy," Monday said materializing next to me. "This dance is a blast. Almost everyone in my old crowd is here."

"Monday's arrived," I told Linda Sue.

"All riiiight." She made a victory sign. "Go get her, bro."

I pretended to talk to Linda Sue, but spoke to Monday. "Have you seen Charlene?"

"No, and I've been looking all over the joint for her. Have you seen any chicks with bangs and a ponytail?"

I shook my head. Boy, Monday was in for a letdown.

He sighed. "What a bummer, as you kids say. My buddies can't see me, and I can't even talk to them. I could have asked if they'd seen Charlene."

"Gee, that is a rotten deal," I said.

"I can't get over how old everyone looks," he went on. "See that man with the pot belly standing by the punch bowl? That's George Rawlings, Garland's star tight end. The woman who just slapped him on the back is Sarah Thomas. You wouldn't think a person her size was once a cheerleader, would you? Oh, look. See that bald man coming in now? That's Ray Sparks, my old baseball buddy." Monday shook his head. "Times do change."

"It sure seems like it." I summarized Monday's story for Linda Sue.

She stared at her "Monday spot" above my right shoulder. "So, Monday. Are you ready for your big revenge?"

His usual, easy smile seemed forced. "Tell Linda Sue I said, 'No sweat.' "

I did, then squeezed his hand. "I'm so glad you're here. I'm really nervous about this skit."

"Nonsense," he snapped. "You'll do fine."

Monday sure wasn't acting like himself. Being rude wasn't his style.

Linda Sue tapped my shoulder. "Better warn Monday about Charlene."

"What about her?" Monday asked.

I took a deep breath. "It's just that Charlene isn't, she's no longer . . ."

What happened to Charlene?" Monday grabbed his chest. "Did she have an accident? Is she st-still alive?"

"No. I mean, yes. She's just . . ."

The band gave a drumroll, and Mr. Smedley walked on-stage. "Ladies and gentlemen," he announced. "It's time for the evening's entertainment."

The butterflies in my stomach started jitterbugging again. I'd tucked my amulet inside my bra, and now I patted it for luck. The music started, and I was swept onstage belting out a chorus of shoo be doo's. My knees shook so hard the poodle on my skirt danced the Fly with me.

"Way to go, Miranda," Linda Sue shouted. "I knew you had it in you."

Was she kidding? The only thing I had in me was Chronic Klutz syndrome. I checked out my legs as we sang "Blueberry Hill" and almost fell off the stage. I *was* kicking high, and in step with the other girls, too.

When we took our bows, wolf whistles filled the gymna-sium. I waved to Monday, and Linda Sue and I hurried into the girls' locker room. While I changed into Adrienne's for-mal, Linda Sue took the videotape out of her purse.

As we went back into the gym, Monday waved to us. "You're a real trooper," he said. "Why did you poor-mouth about being such an awful dancer?"

"I always was before . . . Ohmigosh. My amulet!"

"What about it?" Monday asked.

I pretended to talk to Linda Sue as I answered him. "I meant my onyx must be magic. Before we went on, I rubbed it and wished I wouldn't klutz out in the skit. And I didn't."

Linda Sue rolled her eyes. "Will you give it a rest?"

"Listen to Linda Sue," Monday said. "You did fine in the skit on your own power. Not because you held a supposedly magic amulet in your hot little hand."

"You're wrong, Monday. Now I'm positive this onyx is my lucky charm."

"Knock it off," Linda Sue said. "Mr. Phillips is about to announce the Spring Dance King and Queen."

Monday glanced over his shoulder as Mr. Phillips walked toward the microphone. "Where in blazes is Charlene?"

I had to tell him. "See that table in front of—?"

"Ladies and gentlemen." Mr. Phillips's voice boomed into the microphone. "It gives me great pleasure to introduce this year's Spring Dance royalty, Julie Phillips and Stormy Kincaid!"

Julie and Stormy paraded onstage, and Mr. Phillips placed a gold crown on each of their heads.

Monday gripped my arm. "I can't go through with my revenge," he said.

I patted his hand. "Sure you can. You just have a bad case of nerves, like I did before the skit."

"You don't understand. I am not going to give my revenge speech. Not tonight, not ever."

Grounded Out

13

"What do you mean you're not giving your revenge speech?" I whispered. "Oh, I get it. April Fools', right?"

Monday shook his head. "This isn't a joke, Miranda," he said as Julie started her dance queen speech. "I'm sorry I didn't tell you sooner, but I didn't want to sound ungrateful after all the help you gave me planning my revenge. See, when I saw all my high school hangouts gone, and my friends so old, it hit me how things change, no matter how much you wish they'd stay the same. The only way your life won't change is if you're dead."

A shiver made me wince. People applauded Julie's speech, and she marched upstage to her "throne," one of three tall chairs draped with red velvet.

Stormy began his speech. He smiled at me, and my heart almost jumped out of my chest. My eyes watched Stormy, but I listened to Monday.

"You told me I was wasting my time getting revenge on someone I couldn't stand," he went on. "You were right. You can't set your life on rewind and bring back the past. Life moves in only one direction, Miranda, and that's forward. So I could't blame Charlene anymore for marrying Floyd. I mean, how could I expect her not to marry anyone else when I was dead?"

"You couldn't." My voice came out barely a whisper.

Monday blinked away the tears filling his eyes. "What it boils down to is if you stay focused on yesterday, you'll miss a lot of todays and tomorrows, which, by the way, aren't as bad as I thought." He took a breath. "Are you sore at me for calling off my revenge?"

I shook my head. Monday's tears were contagious. A bunch were now skidding down my own cheeks.

His easy grin returned. "You know what, Miranda Taylor? You're the *greatest*."

I sniffed, and Linda Sue looked at me. "Oh, Miranda. Watching Stormy with Julie is really getting to you, isn't it?"

I wiped my eyes. "Not this time."

Stormy went to sit on his throne, and Mr. Phillips introduced Charlene. Monday gasped as she floated across the stage. "That's *Charlene*?" he shouted.

Linda Sue punched my arm. "How's Monday reacting to Charlene? Is he totally bummed?"

"Afraid so," I answered.

Charlene accepted a bouquet of roses from Mr. Phillips, then took the microphone. Monday's eyes seemed to carve a path from his sockets straight to hers. And as Charlene gave her speech, she seemed to stare right back at him.

I half expected Monday to leap onstage and carry her off into the sunset. But this was real life, not one of Mom's romance novels.

". . . And so, Garland High School," Charlene said, "thanks

for the memories." While everyone clapped, she nodded a thank-you, then walked toward her throne like Miss America gliding down the runway.

Monday nodded too, as if he now shared a private understanding with his old flame. I guess happily ever afters come in all shapes and sizes.

The band started playing a '50s song. I peeked at Stormy. He slouched in his seat, cleaning his fingernails.

"Monday," I said, "I guess all's well that ends— Oh, no. You ended what you came back to earth for."

"Oh, no," Linda Sue echoed. "Does Monday have to leave now?"

Fresh tears filled my eyes. "But Monday. Your two weeks aren't up yet. You can't go back *now*."

"Don't worry. I'm not." A sort of bittersweet smile slid across his face. "I still have some unfinished business to handle."

"What business?" I sniffed.

"Never you mind."

Someone tapped my shoulder, and Monday's smile turned into a frown.

"Hi, Miranda," Stormy said. "I've been looking for you."

My head swam. With all the gorgeous girls here, Stormy Kincaid searched for me. My love spell must be working!

Linda Sue gave me one of her turned off looks. "Later, you guys. I'm going to check out the eats."

"Since you're preoccupied," Monday said, "I'm going to mosey on over to the eats myself. Maybe they have some chocolate."

I sneaked him an apologetic shrug, but he disappeared without a nod. A dull pain seeped into my chest. I missed Monday already, and he hadn't even left yet.

The band switched from '50s music to '80s slow dance.

Stormy led me onto the floor and pressed me against his chest. My heart beat so fast I was afraid I'd faint.

I followed Stormy's lead, feeling like the magician's assistant who gets sawed in half. Part of me loved being with Stormy, while another part of me longed to be with Monday.

Stormy put his lips above my ear, and shivers gyrated inside me. "You're sure different tonight from the girl who bumped into me at the pizza parlor," he said, easing me around the dance floor. "Like in that skit. You seemed to be the leader, really in charge. Know what I mean?"

I didn't, but if Stormy saw something inside me he liked, I wasn't about to discourage him.

He chuckled.

"What's so funny?" I asked.

"Mrs. Phillips's speech. All that talk about the '50s being so great. One time my mom showed me her high school yearbook. Man, I didn't see one girl I'd want to ask out." Stormy paused to wave at a passing brunette. "And if I'd been a girl back then, I would have puked if one of those nerdy-looking guys even touched me."

"Really?" Monday sure wasn't nerdy looking. "Gee, Stormy, I think '50s guys were kind of funky."

"Are you kidding?" He swiveled his head as another pretty girl danced by. "Trust me, Miranda. Mrs. Phillips's speech was bor-ring."

I was beginning to think Stormy Kincaid was bor-ring. Then he breathed on my neck, and my skin tingled. Well maybe not that boring.

"Let's get some fresh air," he said as the band took a break.

I started to answer him, when Julie appeared out of nowhere and maneuvered herself between Stormy and me.

"Oh, Stormy," she gushed as if I weren't there. "Daddy's going to take our picture together. You know, for Spring Dance Queen and King?"

"Later, Julie. Oh, that reminds me." He took off his Spring Dance King crown. "Here. Hold this for me, will you?"

Julie's mouth fell open, and I shot her a look that said "Na na, na na na." She shot me a look that said "I'd like to murder you."

Stormy and I went outside, and he wrapped his arms around me. I blinked to make sure I wasn't dreaming.

"How about a walk?" Stormy asked and led me behind the gym to the baseball field.

My pulse raced. What if he tried to kiss me? Should I let him? If so, was I supposed to close my eyes? Should I put my arms around him, or just let them dangle at my sides? Should I pucker up? I wished I'd asked Mom these questions. With all the romances she's written, Mom was probably an expert on kissing.

My heart beat faster with every step we took away from the gym. What was the matter with me? I was finally alone with my heart's desire, and I was acting like he was Jack the Ripper.

When we reached the baseball diamond, Stormy pulled me into one of the dugouts and planted his lips on mine. His kiss was rough, not at all like the romantic kisses I'd dreamed about.

"Maybe we should go back now," I said and started out of the dugout.

He grabbed my arm. "Why the iceberg routine? You didn't mind being close to me at the Donkey Kong. That night you squeezed me so tight when we danced I thought I'd choke."

"What? You were the one who squeezed the breath out of *me* at the Donkey Kong."

Stormy scoffed. "What kind of number are you pulling, Miranda? One minute you're rubbing my back and dancing so close to me it would take a lug wrench to pull us apart, and the next minute it's hands off."

I stepped backward, away from him. "I'm not pulling a number on you, Stormy. I was dancing close to you because you were dancing close to me, and I thought you liked me." He stepped toward me, and I moved back another step. "I didn't mean what you think I meant, and I'm sorry if you thought I wanted to, I mean, if you thought I meant . . ."

My thoughts were coming faster than my mouth could speak them as Stormy kept moving toward me, and I kept moving backward away from him.

"Cut the Miss Innocence act," he said. "I didn't bring you on this hike for nothing."

"Oh yeah?" I wished I knew how to give a right to the jaw, because I really itched to slug him. "Well, for your information, Stormy Kincaid, that's just what this hike with you is turning into. A big nothing!" I ran out of the dugout.

"Come back here," he yelled, and ran after me. "No girl teases Stormy Kincaid and gets away with it."

"Get lost, creep." I looked over my shoulder to see how close he was.

"You heard the lady," Monday said, materializing behind Stormy. "Get lost."

"Monday!" I stopped running and grabbed at the pain in my side. "Oh, thank goodness you're here."

A lopsided grin sneaked across Stormy's mouth. "I knew you'd change your mi—iiii," he wailed as Monday wrenched his arms behind his back.

"Smarts, doesn't it?" Monday said.

I clapped my hands. I couldn't help it. "You have my permission to clobber him," I told Monday.

"Who are you talking to?" Stormy struggled to free his arms. "I don't see anyone."

Monday held Stormy's wrists behind his back with one hand and grabbed his shirt collar with his other hand. "You don't need to see me to feel my presence, buddy." He loosened Stormy's tie and dragged him back to the baseball diamond. Then he pushed one end of Stormy's tie through a link in the backstop fence and twisted it into a double knot.

As Monday pulled a handkerchief out of his pocket and tied Stormy's hands behind his back, I knew why people say revenge is sweet.

Stormy tried to break loose from the backstop. "I don't know how you did this, Miranda, but you better untie me or our date tomorrow night is off."

I glared at him. "As far as I'm concerned, our date's been off since you turned into an animal. For the kind of playmate you want, try the zoo. There's a gorilla in there just your type."

Stormy's face turned pink, and his neck bulged out of his collar. We left him ranting how I'd regret not untying him.

I sagged against Monday. Until this moment, I never knew teeth could really chatter.

When we reached the gymnasium, Monday led me to the breezeway connecting the gym to the first-floor classrooms. He opened his arms, and I fell inside them. Even if someone had seen me dancing by myself I wouldn't have cared. I'd never felt so light and graceful in my life.

We stayed on the breezeway dancing close, and it seemed we'd been there only a few minutes when Mr. Smedley announced the last dance.

Monday held me even closer as the band played, and my whole body felt like it was floating. I think I could have flown over the gym and back to my house just on the power of the tingling going on inside me. Then all too soon the music stopped, and it was time to leave.

Adrienne's boyfriend, Ben, drove me, Linda Sue, and an invisible Monday home. After we dropped off Linda Sue, Ben parked in front of our house. Then he and Adrienne headed for the family room to do whatever they do after their dates, which, after my experience with Stormy, I didn't want to know about. Monday and I decided to sit on the front porch where no one would hear us talking.

"How could I fall for a no-good creep like Stormy?" I said. "If being with him is what dating's like, I don't care if I ever go out with another guy."

"Heyyyy." Monday pushed a tangled curl out of my eyes. "Everyone falls for a Stormy at least once in their lives. How else would they know what type of person they *didn't* want to date? Trust me, Miranda. One day a nice boy will ask you out. And when he does, I want you to say yes, and I want you to let yourself have a good time. You dig?"

"I dig." And elephants fly. I wondered if this nice-boy-will-ask-you-out routine was another one of Monday's jokes. But the face he turned to me was serious.

"Remember when we were talking about how everything changes?" he asked. "Well, you and I have changed, too, while I was on earth."

My heart stopped. *Was* on earth. "You're leaving, aren't you?"

"I have to."

Tears flooded my eyes. "Wh-when?"

He took my hand. "Tomorrow."

Good-byes, Hellos, and Great Balls of Fire

14

"Please stay one more day," I begged Monday. "Just twenty-four hours?" I paced my room, while Monday sat on the edge of my bed.

"My two weeks are up," he said. "Today is Saturday, and at twelve o'clock tonight it will be exactly two weeks since I met you at Dreamland Cemetery."

"How could two weeks pass so fast? We barely have two hours left together." My throat tightened, and I felt tears sting my eyes.

Monday patted a space next to him on my bed. I stopped pacing and sat down.

"I wish we had more time together, too," he said. "But my mission on earth is over. There's no reason for me to hang around anymore."

"There's *me* to hang around for."

"Aw, Miranda. Try to see things from my point of view. Like that old saying, 'Stand in someone else's shoes.' "

Monday's words reminded me of something I wanted to do before we left for the cemetery. Just thinking of Dreamland sent the tears I'd held back all day spilling down my cheeks.

"Don't cry, Miranda," Monday said. "Can't you see I don't fit in on earth anymore? My ways are 1950s, and yours are the present and beyond."

"So what? Nothing matters to me if you aren't here."

Monday lifted my chin to face him. "Do you think I could leave if I didn't know you'd be okay without me?" The corner of his mouth twitched, showing a hint of a grin. "Besides, I made some arrangements."

"What arrangements? When did you ever have time to . . . Michael Oliver Newberry. Is that what you were doing all those times you disappeared on *spiritual business*?"

The hint of a grin I saw before slithered full-blown across his face. "Let's just say I wasn't out haunting houses." He held up his hands. "Don't ask. You'll find out soon enough."

I looked at Madame Lulu's book lying on my nightstand. "How do you go back up there, anyway? Do you need a spell?"

Monday shrugged. "Nobody up there told me how to return, but I imagine I'll just disappear at midnight, sort of dematerialize for . . . good." His eyes clouded over.

I felt mine doing the same. "Maybe I should bring my amulet."

He lifted an eyebrow. "Bring it if you want. Just remember what I said about magic coming from within you."

From within me. Even that rat Stormy said I looked like I was another person inside during the Spring Dance skit.

Monday took off his letter sweater and crawled under my bed. He emerged dragging his Garland yearbook. "I couldn't forget my yearbook. Or my present for you."

"Really?" I wondered where he'd gotten the money for a gift and prayed he hadn't stolen anything.

"In my day," Monday said, "when a boy cared about a

girl, he gave her his letter sweater. I want you to have mine." He draped the sweater around my shoulders.

I buried my face in its fuzzy collar and smelled chocolate. "Oh, Monday. Thank you. This is the most wonderful present in the whole entire world."

He touched the letter *G* on the pocket. "This gift comes with a condition, Miranda. I want you to promise you won't let your high school years sneak by without taking part in every minute of them. If you hide out in your room and never risk making new friends, or trying out new experiences, I guarantee that later on you'll regret it so much." He seemed to look inside my soul. "Take it from an old spirit who didn't choose to miss out on anything. You'll never have such a carefree time in your life."

His pale blue eyes were like two laser beams shining into me. "I promise," I whispered.

Monday's eyes strayed to the alarm clock on my nightstand. "It's time to leave," he said.

My heart fell to my stomach. For a minute, my legs wouldn't budge. "I'll get my backpack," I said when I could speak without crying.

"Good. I'll check if everyone's asleep."

The second Monday went down the hall I hurried into my closet, relieved that he'd unknowingly reminded me about my gift for him. I put the present in my backpack and grabbed my flashlight.

"All quiet down the hall," Monday announced.

I stuffed my pillows under my blankets so if anyone came into my room they'd think I was asleep. Monday took my hand, and we sneaked out of the house.

Neither of us spoke on the way to Dreamland. When we reached the cemetery, Monday tried the gate. Like the last time, it was padlocked.

"Never fear," he said. "Your spirit is here." He bent his knees and stooped over. "Climb aboard."

I did and my stomach double-flipped as Monday flew us over the fence. I giggled in spite of what was going to happen here. When I slid off his back, a wind I hadn't felt before circled my neck and blew a cloud over the moon.

Monday led me between the rows of graves until we reached his tombstone. Then he put his hands on my arms and stared at me. The look in his eyes made me excited, afraid, and happy, all at the same time.

"Great balls of fire, I'm going to miss you." Slowly, he bent down and kissed me. Really kissed me.

I didn't worry about what I was supposed to do. I just wrapped my arms around him and kissed him back.

When we pulled apart, Monday's chocolate odor grew weaker, and a chill meshed itself into my heart. I dug into my backpack for my amulet, and felt Monday's gift. "Monday, wait. You can't leave without your going away present. Here."

Monday's face lit up like the Fourth of July. "Jeepers! White bucks!" He bolted over to me, kicking off his blue suede shoes along the way. "Where did you ever find them?"

"Remember those buckskins you eyed at the swap meet?"

"Oh, Miranda. You are one crafty female." He slipped on the shoes and swung me in a circle, then suddenly put me down. "I'm sorry, Miranda, but time's run out."

He picked up his blue suede shoes and stood beside his tombstone. All of a sudden his body started to fade.

I tore into my backpack for my magic amulet. "Make Monday stay on earth," I chanted, rubbing the onyx between my fingers. "Make Monday stay on earth."

I looked at Monday. He'd faded until the contours of his body were just an outline. "Oh no, why isn't my amulet working?" I rubbed the onyx harder. "Come on, make him stay, darn you!" I might as well have rubbed a dead leaf.

Monday's feet faded and then vanished completely. From his ankles up, his body kept disappearing as if he were being swallowed by quicksand. His shins vanished, and he floated on his knees.

My soul turned over. The horrible dream I'd had when Monday disappeared was replaying in front of me. But this time my nightmare was real.

"NOOOO!" I cried and ran to Monday. "Stop it! Monday, please come back!"

He didn't answer. His pale blue eyes clouded over as his thighs and stomach vanished. All that remained of my Monday were his chest, his arms, and his head, his corn-silk hair shining in the moonlight.

I grabbed his arms, but my fingers slipped through them. In slow motion, as if it were a struggle, Monday opened his mouth. "Don't cry . . . iii . . . iii." His words echoed across the cemetery. "I'll be around . . . ound . . . ound. See ya later, alligator. . . . After 'while, crocodile . . . ile . . . ile . . . ile. . . ." Monday vanished. And there was no more chocolate smell.

"Monnnnday!" I fell on his tombstone and cried until I felt as if my heart had crumbled into a million pieces.

Then I pulled myself up over the fence and ran out of Dreamland Cemetery. I didn't stop running until I got home. I dragged myself upstairs to my room, not even caring if my folks caught me sneaking into the house in the middle of the night. Being grounded didn't bother me. I didn't want to leave the house anyway with Monday gone.

And in my house is just where I stayed for the rest of spring vacation. All I did was think about Monday and how much I missed him. I hugged his letter sweater and tried to smell the chocolate odor, but it had disappeared, like Monday. I told my folks I'd bought the sweater at a garage sale. There was no way I could tell them about Monday.

Linda Sue came over once, and when I told her how Monday vanished, she started crying, which set me off again.

I rubbed my onyx amulet and wished as hard as I could that Monday would come back. But not even a trace of chocolate filtered into my room. I could almost hear Monday saying, "That amulet's not worth a plugged nickel in the magic department. You have to make your wishes come true yourself."

Monday's words made me start thinking about all the times I'd used my amulet. It was true that even though I'd rubbed my amulet before taking the algebra test I made a B+ on, I'd also really studied for that test. On the other hand, I'd barely cracked a book for the math test I made a D on, when I forgot to bring my amulet to school.

The day before school started, I wrapped the onyx in tissue paper and put it into an envelope. Then I wrote a letter:

Dear Mr. Ogelthorpe,

I'm returning your amulet. I'm sorry I didn't give it back to you sooner, but I thought I needed it. Now I know the amulet can't give me what I want, or make me happy. I'll have to do that myself.

Sincerely,
Miranda Taylor

On the way to school the next morning, I dropped the envelope into the mailbox. I felt sad all day. Last period my mind was still on Monday as I trudged into biology lab.

Mr. Bunyon, fully recovered from the frog episode, was writing an assignment on the board. Yuck. No way was I in the mood to dissect whatever species came after frogs.

When I saw Monday's and Charlene's initials carved in the table, I almost burst into tears. I traced my finger around the *M*.

"Attention, class," Mr. Bunyon said. "Raise your hand if the place next to you is vacant, so our new students can find a seat."

Kids I never saw before spread out between the rows of tables. They must be the students Mr. Bunyon told us about whose school was closing. Nobody sat on my right, so I raised my hand.

A boy with brown hair slung his backpack over the chair next to me. He took out a notebook, a pencil, a biology book, and a handful of candy. "I'm a total basket case without my chocolate," he said.

My heart stopped. Hershey's Kisses.

He grinned. "Want one?"

I almost fell off my chair. The boy had pale blue eyes.

"Ummmm," he said. "Hershey's Kisses are my favorite." He popped the chocolate into his mouth. "Sure you don't want one?"

I just stared at him.

"What's wrong?" he asked. "Is my hair messed up?" He whipped a comb from his back pocket and ran it through his thick, brown hair.

If he'd been blond, I *would* have fallen out of my seat. "Uh, your name wouldn't be Monday, would it?" I asked him.

He cocked his head. "Where'd you get that idea? My name is Thomas Ulysses Edward Stephens. But you can call me by my nickname." His grin stretched to both earlobes. "It's Tuesday."

Outside the window, a fluffy cloud floated across an otherwise clear sky. Arrangements, huh? I smiled. See ya later, alligator. Hardy har har.

ABOUT THE AUTHOR

Author HERMA SILVERSTEIN says: "I wrote *Mad, Mad Monday* mainly to entertain, but also to show today's teenagers some of the highlights of the '50s. And it was fun for me to go back in memory and relive those happy days. While I was writing the book, I enjoyed playing old record albums and watching reruns of '50s television shows."

Ms. Silverstein has written several nonfiction books for young people. She grew up in Texas and now lives in Santa Monica, California, with her two teenage sons.